The PROTECTOR'S PROMISE

Shirlee McCoy

Published by Steeple Hill Books™

STEEPLE HILL BOOKS

ISBN-13: 978-0-373-44314-7
ISBN-10: 0-373-44314-5

THE PROTECTOR'S PROMISE

This edition published by arrangement with Steeple Hill Books.

www.SteepleHill.com

Printed in U.S.A.

Books by Shirlee McCoy

Love Inspired Suspense

Die Before Nightfall
Even in the Darkness
When Silence Falls
Little Girl Lost
Valley of Shadows
Stranger in the Shadows
Missing Persons
Lakeview Protector
**The Guardian's Mission*
**The Protector's Promise*

*The Sinclair Brothers

Steeple Hill Trade

Still Waters

SHIRLEE McCOY

has always loved making up stories. As a child, she daydreamed elaborate tales in which she was the heroine—gutsy, strong and invincible. Though she soon grew out of her superhero fantasies, her love for storytelling never diminished. She knew early that she wanted to write inspirational fiction, and began writing her first novel when she was a teenager. Still, it wasn't until her third son was born that she truly began pursuing her dream of being published. Three years later she sold her first book. Now a busy mother of four, Shirlee is a homeschool mom by day and an inspirational author by night. She and her husband and children live in Washington State and share their house with a dog and a guinea pig. You can visit her Web site at www.shirleemccoy.com.

"Do you think the sheriff has found anything?"

Honor's voice was calm, without the anxiety he'd seen in her eyes.

"If he has, he'll let us know," Grayson replied.

"Hopefully soon. The girls are scared. I want to be able to tell them everything will be okay."

"Who will tell you that, Honor?"

She met his eyes. "I'm an adult. I don't need anyone to." She stepped out into the cold, cutting off their conversation.

Grayson followed, tensing when he saw the sheriff's grim expression. He'd found something.

"Ms. Malone, can you come with me, please?"

Honor walked toward the sheriff, aware of Grayson's gaze as she did so. His intense focus was as warm as a physical caress, tempting her to reach back, take his hand, allow the support he'd offered.

She wouldn't.

Not even for tonight.

She wouldn't allow herself to depend on him. That could only lead to heartache.

For when your faith is tested, your endurance has a chance to grow. So let it grow, for when your endurance is fully developed, you will be strong in character and ready for anything.

—*James* 1:3–4

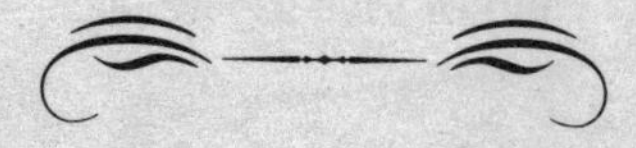

To Sara. The darker the night,
the more beautiful the sunrise.

And in loving memory of Willetta Ruth Pothier
who once told me that I had capable hands.
I didn't understand then. I do now. May I prove
to be as capable of sacrifice, of service
and of love as she was.

ONE

Something woke Honor Malone from deep sleep, the scratchy scrape of it pulling her from dreams of the green hills and cool mists of her native Ireland. She lay silent for a moment, listening to the old bungalow settling and to the quiet whisper of her daughter's breath. Neither was the thing that had woken her. Something else had dragged her from peaceful sleep. She sat up, her heart pounding, her mind racing with images she'd rather forget—a dark shadow, a knife, blood.

The past, she reminded herself. That was in the past, now.

She was in a new home in a new neighborhood. There was nothing to be afraid of. No way that the ugliness that had touched her life could have followed her from St. Louis. She probed the shadows anyway, searching the room for anything out of place. Moving boxes stood against one wall waiting to be unpacked. Her nurse's uniform hung from a hook on the closed bedroom door. Outside, the wind howled, pushing through the cracks in the house's old windowpanes and leaving the air in the room chilly and damp.

Honor shoved aside the heavy quilt her mother had sent as a housewarming gift and stood shivering in her flannel pajamas. Her daughter lay in the bed across the room, and Honor went to her, wanting to assure herself that the four-year-old was okay. Lily lay on her side, sleeping deeply. Safe. Cocooned in blankets and sheets. Just as she should be.

A soft scraping sound froze Honor in place, the noise discordant against the backdrop of wind. Scrape. Tap. Scrape. Like a stick scratching against the window.

Or a knife.

Fear raced up her spine and refused to leave, no matter how many times she told herself that the sound was nothing but the branch of one of the old rosebushes butting up against the window. Her feet moved in slow motion as she walked toward the sound, her stomach hollow with terror. She wanted to climb back into bed, pull the thick comforter over her head and pretend she hadn't heard anything, but she had a family—her daughter and her sister-in-law—to protect. She'd face anything to keep them safe.

Her hand shook as she eased back the curtains and peered outside, bracing herself for whatever she might see. All she saw was darkness pressing against the glass and wispy tendrils of fog that danced eerily in the yard, swirling and swaying, concealing and revealing as the wind blew them away.

Was something else moving out there?

Honor leaned close to the window, squinting as she tried to find substance in the mist.

Scrape.

She jumped back, her heart racing so fast she was surprised it didn't leap from her chest.

Scrape. Tap.

A branch. It had to be. She hadn't seen anything else at the window. She pulled back the curtains again, this time looking down. Overgrown rosebushes brushed against the house with every gust of wind, their gnarled branches tapping against the aluminum siding. That's what she'd heard. Nothing sinister. Nothing frightening. Nothing to get herself worked up about.

She sighed, dropping the curtains and crossing the room. Her shift at Lakeview Haven Assisted Living facility had ended at two, and she'd been home fifteen minutes later. Exhausted, she should have been asleep as soon as her head hit the pillow, but Honor had tossed and turned until after three. Now, it was nearly six and she was awake again.

She knew she should climb back into bed and try to get back to sleep, but the dream had reminded her of things she'd rather forget. Longings and disappointments. Joy and bitter sorrow.

She eased open the bedroom door, closing it quietly before crossing the hall and hesitating in front of her sister-in-law's room. Candace was years past needing to be checked on. But knowing that didn't keep Honor from pushing open the door and peeking into the room. The golden glow of a night-light illuminated the bed where Candace lay. At eighteen, she should have been too old to need the light, but she'd never outgrown it. Despite her maturity, Candy's childhood still haunted her dreams. Honor had given up trying to broach the subject. Instead, she'd done what Candace preferred and learned to pretend that the past wasn't still alive in her sister-in-law's mind.

Honor retreated, closing the door and walking down the hall, knowing she wouldn't be getting any more sleep. The past month had been filled with traumas large and small. Honor had hoped that moving to Lakeview, Virginia, would help settle the family back into the normal rhythm of life, but leaving St. Louis had been much harder than she'd expected.

Harder on Honor.

Harder on Candy.

Harder on Lily, who had only ever known their tiny apartment in the busy city. Lily, who thought that everyone should marry a prince and live in a castle. Lily who had her father's dreams shining in her eyes.

The thought had the same bitter sting it always did, but Honor pushed it aside. She didn't have time to waste mourning the past. Her girls were her priority. Her job, her faith were what pulled them all through the difficult times. This time would be no different.

She turned on the light in the small outdated kitchen, moving quietly as she put a kettle of water on the stove and pulled a tea bag from the canister on the counter. The window above the sink looked over the backyard, and again and again her eyes were drawn to the gray predawn scene. In the city, there had always been light and noise. Here, it was almost too quiet. Too dark. She'd get used to it eventually, she supposed. Just as she'd adapted to city life after living for years in the lush Irish countryside.

She smiled a little as she remembered the childhood years she'd spent exploring the beauty of God's creation with her friends. Those memories were one of the reasons she'd moved to a small town in a rural area. The other reason was Candace's decision to attend a Christian college in Lynchburg. Honor had wanted to stay close to her sister-in-law.

She'd also wanted to escape the memories that didn't seem to want to let her go.

A cup of tea in hand, she walked into the small mudroom off the kitchen, grabbed her coat from the rack and shoved her bare feet into boots. Cold mist kissed her skin as she stepped outside. A few yards away from the back door, an old swing set stood neglected and worn, its skeletal limbs planted firmly in moist earth. Honor took a seat on a wooden swing, nursing the hot teacup in her hand, the still, quiet morning enveloping her. The silence of it, the beauty, carried her away from the anxiety that had been dogging her for weeks and muffled the wordless demands that had become almost too much for Honor to meet. Here, in the peaceful moments before the day began, she could finally hear the quiet voice of her Creator, whispering that everything would be okay.

A muted sound broke the silence. A branch snapping? Honor tensed, scanning the yard, her gaze finally caught and held by movement at the far end of the property. A line of shrubs separated her yard from the one behind it, and Honor was sure something had moved there. As she watched, a dark figure stepped into view. Tall. Broad-shouldered. Brown hair. Those were the only details she could make out.

All the details she *needed* to make out.

The teacup dropped from her fingers, shattering on the ground as she raced toward the safety of the house.

Grayson Sinclair called himself fifteen kinds of fool as he followed the fleeing figure across Oliver Silverton's overgrown backyard. A squatter, probably. Someone who'd learned that the ramshackle place was empty and had decided to call it home for a night or two.

It wasn't Grayson's business, of course. Oliver had made it clear that he didn't want help taking care of his property. Nor was he open to advice on how best to get the dilapidated house rented out.

After three years of living back to back with the property,

Grayson had given up trying to help the old man who owned it. Still, when he'd glimpsed a light shining from a back window, he'd decided to investigate.

More to help himself than to help his neighbor.

The fact was, after two weeks of standing vigil over his brother's hospital bed, wondering if Jude was going to live or die, Grayson needed something else to focus on. A problem he could actually solve.

A brother in New York, facing months of physical therapy and an uncertain future?

That he couldn't fix.

A squatter in Oliver Silverton's house?

Grayson could take care of that problem, and quickly.

He strode to the back door, the anger he felt out of proportion to the squatter's crimes. He knew where his anger was really directed—at the hit-and-run driver who'd slammed into Jude while he'd been out of his car helping a stranded motorist.

Grayson turned the doorknob to the old house, expecting it to open as it had a few months ago when he'd put a stop to a group of kids who'd decided to have a party on the premises. To his surprise, the door was locked. A shadow passed in front of the window and the light spilling from it went out.

Did the squatter really think that would convince him to leave?

Grayson slammed a fist against the door, not worried about the force he was using. Not caring. The person inside the house had better open up and explain himself. Grayson wasn't leaving until he did. "Open up. This is private property and you're trespassing."

There was no response, and Grayson pulled out his cell phone, determined to handle the problem with the same efficient ease with which he prosecuted criminals. He couldn't help his brother, but he *could* do this.

And he would.

The phone rang once before Grayson's friend Sheriff Jake Reed picked up. "Reed, here."

"It's Grayson. There's a trespasser in Silverton's place again."

"When'd you get back from New York?"

"Half an hour ago."

"And you're at the Silverton place now?"

"Yeah, trying to kick out the trespasser, but he's locked in and won't budge."

Jake laughed, the sound only adding to Grayson's irritation. "Look, maybe you find it funny, but I've had a rough couple weeks and I'm not in the mood to deal with a vagrant who's decided this is home. So, if you don't mind, I'd appreciate you coming over and dealing with it yourself."

"Hey, sorry, man. I know things have been rough. Tiffany and I have been praying for your brother. Most of the people in Lakeview have. How's Jude doing?"

"He'll be in the hospital for another couple of weeks. Then in a rehab facility. It'll be a while before we know if he'll ever walk again."

"I'm sorry."

"Yeah. Me, too. Now, are you coming over here or not?"

"I was already on my way when you called. Seems the new renter thinks someone is trying to break in."

"Renter?" Surprised, Grayson stepped away from the door.

"Moved in last week. A nurse, her daughter and sister-in-law."

"No husband?"

"Nope. Rumor has it, he's deceased, but I haven't actually met the woman or heard the truth from her."

"She was out in the yard and saw me coming through the shrubs that separate our property. I must have scared her half to death." Grayson's anger fled, and he glanced at the darkened window. He could picture the poor woman cowering just out of sight, a phone clutched to her ear as she prayed the police would arrive before he broke down the door. He had a vivid image in his head—a woman in her forties or fifties. Widowed with a teenage daughter and an older sister-in-law who lived with them. Short. Round. Salt-and-pepper curls.

Terrified.

"You scared her enough that she called nine-one-one. I'll have my dispatcher tell her you're a concerned neighbor and there's nothing to worry about. See you in a few." Jake hung up, and Grayson hesitated. Should he knock again? Walk away? What was the protocol for this kind of thing?

Before he could decide, the door cracked open, an old-fashioned chain pulled tight across the space. "Grayson Sinclair?"

"That's right."

"It appears we're neighbors, then." Her voice held a touch of Ireland, its husky timbre reminding Grayson of cool fall evenings and warm laughter.

"It appears so. I'm sorry for frightening you. I've been out of town for a couple of weeks and hadn't heard the place had been rented out."

"And I'm sorry for calling the police on you. I get nervous when strangers chase me across the yard. Hold on." She closed the door, and Grayson could hear the chain sliding free. When she opened it again, he caught his breath in surprise.

His new neighbor was not in her forties or fifties.

Not round.

Not sporting salt-and-pepper curls.

Not anything like he'd imagined her to be.

"I'm Honor Malone, Mr. Sinclair. It's good to meet you. Despite the circumstance." Her half smile pulled Grayson's attention to lips that were soft and full.

He jerked his gaze to her eyes, irritated with himself. Obviously, driving all night had left him a few brain cells short of clear thinking. "It's good to meet you, too. Jake didn't say when you'd moved in."

"A week ago. Mr. Silverton mentioned that the place had been empty for a long time. I'm not surprised you were worried about squatters."

"We have had a problem with vagrants a few times over the years. That and kids using the house as a party resort."

"Let's hope that you won't have either problem again. Come in and have a cup of coffee while we wait for the sheriff." She turned and walked through the tiny mudroom, not bothering to wait for his response.

Grayson followed, intrigued by Honor Malone despite the voice whispering in his head and reminding him that he'd washed his hands of relationships and women months ago.

He paused at the threshold of the kitchen, impressed by the changes he saw. Honor had already begun making the old bungalow into a home. Layers of grime had been scrubbed from the countertops, revealing bright blue vintage tiles. The faded wood floor had taken on a high shine that must have taken hours of labor. Cabinets that Grayson would have been willing to testify under oath were beyond salvaging, were now a bright white.

"The place looks great." He spoke out loud, and Honor turned to face him, her cheerful yellow flannel pajamas at odds with the strain he saw in her face. Despite her smile, she looked worn, her eyes deeply shadowed.

"Thank you. It's been a labor of love."

"It's a lot of work to put into a rental property."

"Not if you're renting to own." She grabbed coffee cups from the cupboard, the sleeves of her pajamas falling back to reveal delicate wrists. Her fingers were long and slender, her left hand bare.

"You plan to buy this place?" The surprise in his voice must have been obvious, because Honor stiffened.

"Is there some reason why I shouldn't?"

"It's…" Neglected? Past hope? A money pit? "Going to take a lot of work."

"What doesn't, Mr. Sinclair?"

"It's Grayson, and you've got a point. Most things worth having take hard work to achieve."

"I told myself that a hundred times while I was removing layers of wax from this floor." She smiled, her face going from girl-next-door pretty to stunning in the beat of heart.

More intrigued than ever, Grayson studied her face. Heart-shaped with high cheekbones dusted with freckles. Full lips and wide green eyes tilted at the corners. Not conventionally beautiful. There was something there, though. Something that made him want to keep looking.

"What?" She frowned, her cheeks turning scarlet.

"I was expecting a drifter. Instead, I found a beautiful woman."

"And I was expecting an intruder and instead found a man who knows how to turn a sweet phrase." She busied herself gathering mugs, cream and sugar. Apparently not at all impressed by his flattery.

He supposed that was for the best. He wasn't in the market for a relationship. Even if he were, flattery wasn't the way he'd pursue one. He believed in the direct approach.

A soft knock saved Grayson from having to reply to Honor's comment. Jake. Finally. Grayson could offer another apology to his friend, then be on his way. His life was already complicated enough. He didn't need to add more trouble to the mix.

And something told him that's exactly what Honor Malone would be if he let her—trouble.

Compelling, alluring, distracting trouble.

TWO

Honor hurried through the dining room and living room, sure that she could feel Grayson's steady gaze on her back. His eyes were the bright blue of the flowers that had bloomed in her mother's garden every spring. Looking in them had been like coming home.

Frustrated by her foolish thoughts, she yanked the door open, not sure how she had gone from enjoying a hot cup of tea alone to making coffee for a good-looking, smooth-talking man.

"Next time you might want to ask who it is." A dark-haired stranger stood on the porch, his hard face shadowed by the dim morning light, his sheriff's uniform shouting his identity.

"I knew you were coming, so—"

"You can never be sure who is standing on the other side of the door, ma'am. It may not always be who you're expecting."

"I know. I guess with everything that has happened this morning, I wasn't thinking clearly. You are Sheriff Reed, right?" She knew her face was three shades of red, but Honor tried to smile anyway.

"That's right. And you're Honor Malone."

"Come on in." Honor stepped back, allowing the sheriff to move into the living room. "The dispatcher said you were coming out to make sure everything had been cleared up with my neighbor."

"And to meet you. This is a small town, and I make it a habit to say hello to people when they move in." He didn't even crack a smile when he said it, and Honor wondered if his reasons for meeting new people were altruistic or if he just wanted to add to his list of potential suspects.

She didn't dare ask.

"I've just made a pot of coffee. Would you like a cup?" It seemed like the right thing to say, but Honor couldn't help hoping that the sheriff would refuse her offer. Two men standing in her kitchen drinking coffee was two more than Honor could handle.

"A cup of coffee would be good right about now. Thanks."

Wonderful.

She led the sheriff toward the back of the house, sure he was noticing every detail of the cluttered living and dining rooms—the still-packed moving boxes, the faded furniture and dusty floors. The peeling wallpaper that she planned to pull down as soon as she had a spare minute. Lily's crayons were scattered across the dining room table. Candace's textbooks were piled on a chair.

In the past week, Honor had spent all her time making the kitchen warm and inviting. In her mind, it was the heart of the home, the place where the family gathered to share in each other's lives. The sheriff wouldn't know that, though, and would probably think the chaos was a normal part of Honor's daily life.

"I'm really sorry about the mess, Sheriff Reed. We just moved in a week ago, and I had to start my job two days later. Things have been hectic and…"

Her voice trailed off as she stepped into the kitchen. The room was a lot more crowded than it had been a few minutes ago. Not only was Grayson still there, but Candace and Lily had joined him. The first wore faded jeans and a sweatshirt, her blond hair pulled back into a sleek ponytail. The second wore pink-and-red-striped tights, a pink tutu, an orange sweater and a baseball cap. Both were looking at Grayson as if he were a fairy-tale prince come to life.

Appalled, Honor strode across the room, deciding to deal with the only problem she could. Her daughter's attire. "Lily Mae Malone, what in the world are you wearing?"

"My princess clothes." Lily met Honor's gaze with wide-eyed innocence, her curly brown hair brushing against cheeks still baby-smooth and chubby. At four years old she was only just beginning to lose the baby look, her bright eyes and bowed lips making her look like a mischievous cherub.

"You know better than to entertain guests dressed like that. Now, march back to your room and put on something else."

"But—"

"Go. Now. Before you lose your library privileges." It was the worst threat she could make, and Lily's eyes widened even more. Precocious and imaginative, Lily had begun reading at three and liked nothing better than to check out books of fairy tales from the library.

"I'll help her find something." Candace spoke quietly. Her eyes—so similar in color and shape to Lily's—were much more somber than her younger counterpart's. She shot a last look in Grayson's direction before taking Lily's hand and hurrying her from the room.

"I'm so sorry if the girls were bothering you, Grayson. We haven't been here long enough for Lily to make friends, and

Candace has been busy with her college schedule. They were both probably anxious for a little change in the new routine." Honor grabbed another mug, poured coffee and handed a cup to the sheriff.

"They weren't bothering me. And your sister-in-law isn't really a girl." Grayson stood near the mudroom door, his hip leaning against the counter, a coffee cup in his hand. Light brown hair fell to just below his collar and a hint of stubble shadowed his jaw. He looked rugged and outdoorsy. Exactly the kind of guy Honor would have taken note of years ago.

But this wasn't years ago, and she'd decided after Jay's death that her days of noticing men, of dating them, of falling in love were over. She'd had enough of all three to last a lifetime. "No, she isn't. She'll be nineteen in a few months."

"You said she was a college student. Is she attending Liberty University?"

"Why do you want to know?" Honor's question came out much more abruptly than she'd intended it to. A month ago, Grayson's curiosity wouldn't have seemed odd. Now she was suspicious of everyone.

"Because he can't leave his work at the office," Sheriff Reed answered, a touch of amusement in his voice and a half smile easing the harsh angles of his face.

"His work?"

"He's a prosecuting attorney for the state of Virginia. And he's never met a question he didn't want to ask."

"Guilty as charged." Grayson flashed a dimple Honor hadn't noticed before and shouldn't be noticing now. "Sorry. Sometimes my curiosity gets the best of me. Although this time I had a good reason for asking. We've got several teens in the community who are attending

Liberty. I thought Candace might like to meet them if she's attending the same school."

"She is." Feeling foolish, Honor stirred two spoonfuls of sugar into her coffee and topped it off with a dollop of cream. She was suspicious of everyone lately and knew she shouldn't be.

"I'll give the kids a heads-up. Maybe they can stop by one day."

"That's very kind of you."

"It's no problem." He raised an eyebrow as she spooned more sugar into her coffee, but didn't comment.

"And I may be able to hook your daughter up with a play date or two. How old is she?" The sheriff broke into the conversation, and Honor gladly pulled her attention away from Grayson.

"Four going on forty."

"Mine is three going on thirty. They probably have a lot in common."

"I think they probably do. Would either of you like a biscuit to go with your coffee? I'm sure I've got shortbread." She opened the cupboard closest to her and stretched to reach the box of biscuits on the top shelf.

"Let me." Grayson grabbed it from her hands, his fingers brushing hers. It had been a long time since a man had helped her like that, and Honor's cheeks heated, her heart jumping in silent acknowledgment.

"Thank you. The biscuits are from Ireland. My mother sends them every few months because she knows how much I enjoy them." She opened the box of biscuits, biting her lip to keep from saying more. The last thing she wanted to do was babble on about biscuits when what she should really be doing was hurrying the men through their coffee and out of her house. With Grayson on her left and the sheriff on her right, Honor was boxed in. Out-sized and outnumbered by two men who seemed to be taking up more than their fair share of space.

"Ireland, huh? I thought I heard a bit of Irish brogue in your voice." Grayson took a biscuit from the open box she held out to him, smiling his thanks.

And what a smile it was.

Stunningly warm and inviting, begging Honor to relax and enjoy the moment.

"Yes, well, it's faded a lot since I arrived in the States thirteen years ago. Would you like one?" She held the box out to the sheriff, but he shook his head, setting his mug in the sink.

"Actually, I've got to head out. Thanks for the coffee, Mrs. Malone. It was nice meeting you."

"Thank you for coming out for a false alarm. I'll see you out." She set her coffee down, but Sheriff Reed shook his head.

"No need. I can see myself out. Grayson, you take care of yourself. Keep us updated on your brother's progress. Tiffany and I will keep the prayer loop going as long as necessary."

"Thanks. My family and I appreciate that more than you know."

His brother was ill?

Honor wanted to ask, but she was sure that would qualify as getting involved in Grayson's life. And that was something she was certain she didn't want to do.

Of course, she knew she would do it anyway.

As soon as Sheriff Reed walked out the back door, she turned to her visitor, noting the shadows beneath his eyes and the tension bracketing his mouth. Now that she knew something had happened to his brother, she saw the evidence of his worry clearly. Whatever was going on, it had to be big. "You said you were out of town for a couple of weeks? Was that because of your brother?"

If he was bothered by her question, his expression didn't show it. "I'm afraid so. Jude was nearly killed by a hit-and-run driver two weeks ago. Both his legs were crushed, his back was broken and his spinal cord was affected. Add that to head trauma, and you've got injuries that were barely survivable. Jude is stabilized now, but it was touch-and-go for several days."

"I'm so sorry."

"Yeah. Me, too. My brother is a homicide detective in New York City. A good one. That's been his passion for as long as I can remember. Now he isn't sure if he'll ever be able to return to work."

"That's terrible. Is there anything I can do besides pray for him?"

"Unless you can assure him that he'll be up on his own two feet, running and climbing and working like he used to, no."

"I wish I could do that, but the prognoses on spinal cord injuries are as varied as the injuries themselves. That, combined with the injuries to your brother's legs, will give him a long row to hoe, but if the spinal cord wasn't severely damaged then there's every chance your brother will walk again."

"So the doctors said, but it's two weeks after the injury and Jude still has residual paralysis."

"Two weeks out isn't as long as it seems. I've seen people regain nerve function all at once. I've seen others regain it slowly over the course of weeks and even months. Don't let your brother give up hope."

Grayson grabbed another biscuit from the box, eyeing Honor with steady intent. "I'd forgotten that Jake said you were a nurse."

"Should I ask how he knew that since we'd never met?"

"News travels fast here in Lakeview."

"I'll have to keep that in mind."

"Why? Is there something you'd rather people around here not know?" He raised a dark eyebrow, and Honor laughed, hoping he didn't sense the truth. Of course there were things she'd rather keep to herself. Like the fact that she'd been attacked and nearly killed a month ago. Or that the death of the drug user who'd broken into her apartment had been headline news.

"Just that my daughter believes in fairy tales and that she's constantly looking for a prince."

"In that case, your secret is safe with me." He placed his cup in the sink. "I've got to head out. Thanks for the coffee."

"You're welcome."

"Funny, I had the impression you'd much rather I'd declined your invitation."

Honor's cheeks heated, but she refused to look away from his steady gaze. "Entertaining guests wasn't on my agenda for today."

"But you invited Jake and me anyway."

"It seemed like the right thing to do."

"And you always try to do the right thing?"

"Are you back to prosecutor mode?"

"Actually, this time I was just being a curious neighbor." Grayson smiled, his firm lips curving, his eyes crinkling at the corners. Not a man given to sulking and anger, Honor thought. More the kind to find the fun in the most ordinary of circumstances. It was a good attitude to have, though carried too far it could lead to trouble. Honor had seen enough of that in her husband, Jay, to know just how far a happy-go-lucky attitude could take a person—from the height of success to the depth of ruin and back again.

She grimaced as she hurried through the mudroom and opened the door for Grayson, waving goodbye as he strode across a yard bathed in silvery morning light.

It was for the best that he was leaving, and for the best that Honor avoid seeing him again. She'd fallen for an easygoing, fly-by-night kind of guy once. In the six years she and Jay had been married, she'd been passionately in love with him and, at times, just as passionately frustrated with him. No way would she go through that again. Not for love. Not for companionship. Not for anything. Her girls deserved a stable, secure home. That's exactly what Honor planned to provide for them. Nothing would change that. Not circumstances. Not friendships. And certainly not a good-looking prosecutor whose eyes reminded her of home.

THREE

The next few days passed in a blur of work and chores. Honor's supervisor had worked hard to schedule around Candace's classes, allowing Honor to work four ten-hour shifts. Honor appreciated it, but by the end of the fourth night, she was exhausted, dragging herself to the nurse's station to punch out and praying she had the energy to drive home.

"Are you heading straight home, Honor? Or would you like to go have something to eat and a cup of coffee first?" William Gonzalez glanced up from some paper work he was filing as Honor grabbed her coat and purse. Despite the long shift he'd just worked, Will looked wide awake and raring to go.

"I'm definitely going straight home. I've got a million things to catch up on this weekend. The sooner I get started, the sooner I'll be done."

"I hear you. Maybe we can hook up another time?" He smiled, flashing straight white teeth. At a little over five foot nine, with dark eyes and a compassionate nature, William was the handsome center of romantic attention at Lakeview Haven, and he knew it.

Unfortunately for Will, Honor was much too busy for light flirtation—or anything else, for that matter. Though she had to admit, since she'd met Grayson Sinclair, she'd spent far too much time wondering what it would be like if she *did* have time. Remembering his dimple, his eyes, the warmth of his fingers when they'd brushed against hers…

Stop it!

You are not some teenage girl mooning over a boy. You're a grown woman who's had enough of love to last her a lifetime.

She forced her attention back where it belonged: on her conversation with Will. "My life is pretty hectic right now. I don't have time for much more than work and the girls."

"Too bad. You and I have a lot in common." He smiled again, but there was a tightness to his expression that hadn't been there before. Had her refusal offended him? Honor hoped not. She and Will worked the same shift and she didn't want there to be tension between them.

"The same thing we have in common with all the other nurses here, I'd say. Our jobs." She tried to make light of things as she put on her coat and buttoned it.

"And that we're both far from home. I grew up in Mexico. My entire family is still there. Makes for a lonely life sometimes."

"Lonely?" Honor smiled and hiked her purse up onto her shoulder, knowing that Will was anything but that. "The way I hear it, you keep pretty busy with the other nurses around here. I'm not sure how that adds up to being lonely."

Will laughed and shook his head. "I do like to hang out with some of my co-workers, but that doesn't mean I'm not lonely. Especially on the days I work. These ten-hour shifts are killers when it comes to friendship."

"We do get three days off. I'm sure you find plenty of time

to go out when you're not here. Rumor has it you've dated every nurse here."

"Except for you."

"Which is exactly how I plan to keep it."

"Why?" He seemed sincerely curious, and Honor answered.

"I was married before, Will, and I have a daughter. At this point in my life, I'm not looking to begin another relationship."

"All right. That's cool. Hey, give me a minute to finish filing this paper work and I'll walk you out. It's still dark, and you never know what might be hiding in the shadows."

"The parking lot is well lit, I'll be fine. Thanks for offering, though. See you Tuesday?"

"See you then." He waved and turned his attention back to his filing, leaving Honor to walk down the corridor and into the lobby alone.

The front door opened onto a wide veranda that wrapped around the building and provided a covered area for the residents. Colorful chairs and small tables were spaced carefully to allow room for walkers and wheelchairs. During the day, the area had a serene and cheerful air.

In the dark hours before dawn it was anything but cheerful. Bright overhead lights cast long shadows across the cement floor, creating odd shapes that could have been object, creature or person.

Honor shivered as she hurried toward her car, trying to tell herself there was nothing to be afraid of, but unable to shake her fear. She might have left behind the apartment where she'd been attacked, but the memory still haunted her. Wild eyes peering out from a black ski mask. A knife slashing toward her. The quick, hard beat of her heart as she put her hand up to defend herself and fell backward screaming. The crashing thud of the door as her neighbor kicked it in, running to her rescue with his service revolver in hand, shouting for Honor's attacker to put down the knife. The sharp report of the gun as he'd fired. The soft thud of a body hitting the ground.

Blood.

Everywhere.

Honor shuddered. Thank the Lord Lily and Candace had been at the library. If they'd been home…

She shook her head, refusing to put words to what could have happened. She'd been over it all in her mind during the days that followed the incident. After several sleepless nights, she'd known she had two choices—spend her life reliving the horror she'd experienced or thank God for keeping her family safe and move on. She'd chosen the latter.

Sometimes, though, doing that was harder than it should be.

She pulled open the car door and had started to slide inside when she heard the quiet shuffle of feet on pavement. She glanced around, saw nothing and dropped into her seat, pulling the door closed, locking it against whatever might be lurking in the darkness.

A sharp tap sounded on the back window of the car, and Honor screamed, her hands shaking as she tried desperately to get the key in the ignition. Another knock sounded, this one next to her ear, and she screamed again, turning toward the sound, expecting to look into a ski-masked face.

Instead, she met Will's concerned gaze.

She unrolled the window, fear making her angry. "What in the world are you doing?"

"Bringing you a message." If he realized how afraid she was, he didn't show it.

"A message?"

"Yeah. Janice just called and said we've got a staff meeting Tuesday at noon. It's mandatory. She was going to call you at home, but I told her I thought I could catch you."

"Tuesday at noon? Are you kidding? Our shift doesn't begin until two."

"That's what I told her, but she said we've all got to be there."

"All right. I guess I'll have to work it out."

"See you then." Will waved and strode away.

For a moment after his departure, Honor didn't move. Her hands were too shaky, her legs too weak to drive. She took a deep breath. Then another, forcing oxygen into her lungs, her brain, her limbs. Coming to a small town was supposed to make her feel safer, so why was she jumping at everything?

Frustrated with herself, she put the car into Drive and started toward home, fear still pounding a hollow beat in her throat. "Lord, I need Your help pulling myself together. I can't afford to be afraid all the time. Not when the girls are depending on me. Not when I know You're in control."

She muttered the prayer as she drove along the winding road that led home, the sense of peace she always felt when bringing her problems to God filling her. No matter what her troubles, her faith had always carried her through. These new challenges and new worries would be handled with the same firm trust in God that she'd always had.

And she would get through them.

She would.

She pulled up in front of the bungalow, forcing herself to relax and enjoy the sight of the little house.

A house on a quiet street.

She'd dreamed of it for years, and now she had it. She

wouldn't let the past steal the pleasure of achieving what she'd longed for.

The door creaked as she opened it, the light from a small table lamp welcoming her home. Candace's doing, of course. In the five years since the teenager had moved in with Honor, Candace had worked hard to be a productive member of the family. While other teenagers partied and rebelled, Candace studied hard and helped around the house. After Jay's death, when Honor had been at the end of her pregnancy and overwhelmed with the prospect of raising a child alone, Candace had promised to do whatever she could to help out. She'd been true to her word, never once complaining when she'd had to rush home to babysit Lily while Honor worked. Even now, when she could easily exert her independence, insist on living on campus away from her rambunctious niece, she'd chosen to live at home and continue to help out. Honor would miss her when she finally made her step into independent living.

"Mommy?" Lily's loud whisper came from the dark hall, and Honor tensed. She'd been praying for a few hours of sleep before her little girl woke up. Apparently she wasn't going to get them. She shrugged out of her coat and turned to face her daughter.

"Sweetheart, what are you doing up?"

"I have to tell you something."

"At three-thirty in the morning?"

"It's important, Mommy." Lily bounded toward her, the pink nightgown she wore brushing the floor as she moved, her wild curls bouncing.

Honor lifted her, inhaling the sweet smell of innocence and life. "Okay. So tell me. Then we're both getting into bed."

"I've been thinking about something." Lily put her hand on Honor's face and stared into her eyes, the deep blue of her gaze so similar to Jay's it made Honor's throat tighten.

"About what?"

"About the prince."

Honor bit back impatience and answered in a quiet tone. She and her daughter had had this conversation too many times over the past two days. "Lily Mae, what did we decide before I left for work?"

"That there wasn't a prince."

"Then there's nothing to talk about, is there?"

"But, Mommy, there is. There really truly is. He was right here in our house, and he must be a prince because he lives in that big castle."

"That isn't a castle. It's just a big house. And Mr. Sinclair is not prince. He's a man."

"Princes are men."

Honor sighed, setting her daughter down. "Yes, but not every man is a prince. Some are just men. Some are even frogs dressed up as men."

As she'd hoped, the idea caught her imaginative daughter's attention, and Lily laughed. "You're very silly, Mommy."

"And so are you to be thinking we have a prince living in our backyard."

"Not our backyard. In his house. Only I think it isn't a house. I think it's a castle."

"And I think it is not. So that is the last we'll say about it tonight. Come on. Back to bed with you." She took her daughter's hand and began leading her down the hall, but Lily was her father's daughter, and she wasn't willing to give up her dream.

"Can we go there and visit? Maybe we can find his crown. Then we'll know he's really a prince."

"No, we can not. Mr. Sinclair is a busy man. He doesn't have time to entertain us."

"But—"

"Listen, my sweet, don't the princes in fairy tales always ride white horses?"

"Yes."

"And have you seen any white horses around here?"

"No."

"Then there can't be any princes around, either, can there?" It was twisted logic, but if it worked, Honor would use it.

"Maybe—"

"Maybe we should stop talking and go to sleep."

"But I'm not tired."

Honor shook her head and pressed a finger to her daughter's lips. "Maybe you aren't, but I am. I worked for a very long time today, remember?"

"Yes."

"And now it's time for me to sleep so that I can be ready to do lots of fun things with you and Candace later on."

"Like go to the library?"

"Exactly like that." Honor started down the hall again, stopping when Candace peeked out of her room.

"Is everything okay?" Candace's voice was husky from sleep.

"Yes. Lily just needed to talk to me."

"Not about Prince Sinclair, I hope." Candace wrinkled her nose, and shot a disgruntled look in Lily's direction. "Didn't I tell you not to bug your mother about that?"

"I wasn't, Aunt Candy. Really."

"Yeah? So why are we all awake when we should be

sleeping?" Candace ruffled Lily's hair and met Honor's gaze. "Sorry about this."

"Why should you be sorry? You weren't the one waiting up for me with dreams in your eyes." Honor smiled at her sister-in-law and pushed open the door to the room she shared with Lily.

"Yeah, but I am the one who keeps bringing books of fairy tales home from the library. Listen, why don't you sleep in a little today? I don't have school, so I can watch Lily until you're ready to get up."

"Candace, you've watched her every night this week. I can't ask you to do more."

"You're not asking. We're family. Helping each other is what we do." She smiled, the shadows in her eyes speaking words she wouldn't say. Words about what real family meant to her. About the time she'd spent without the kind of love every child deserves.

"Maybe I will, then, but the rest of the day will be yours to do with as you please."

"Being here pleases me." She smiled again, stepping back into her room and closing the door before Honor could comment.

Honor resisted the urge to knock on the door, make sure Candace was okay, that the shadows in her eyes were gone. Though she'd tried to broach the subject of Candace's childhood many times over the years, what she knew about it could fit on half a sheet of paper.

Jay's mother had inherited a fortune from her father and the family had lived a high-society life in Houston. Money hadn't bought the family happiness, though. Jay's stories of the abuse he'd suffered as a kid had torn at Honor's heart. When his mother had called to ask if Jay's troubled sister could stay with him for a while, Honor had been quick to agree.

Five years later, she didn't regret the decision. Though she wished Jay had been around to see how much his sister had grown, how mature she'd become.

The melancholy thought brought the sadness that always came when Honor thought of Jay. He might have been a happy-go-lucky dreamer with more ideas than plans for achieving them, but they'd been good friends before they married, and had continued to be friends until the day he'd died. "Come on, Lily-girl, let's lie down until the sun comes up."

"When is that?"

"A few hours." Honor tucked Lily under thick blankets, pulling them up around her chin and leaning down to kiss her daughter's forehead.

"Maybe we should have a snack first so we don't get hungry while we sleep."

"I don't think so. Snacks are for times when the sun is up."

"Later?"

"Yes, later. Good night, sweetheart."

"Good morning, Mommy."

Honor smiled and shook her head. Lily was a funny little girl. Advanced for her age and filled with imagination, she kept Honor and Candace on their toes. For now, though, she seemed to be content to lie in bed quietly. Perhaps she was hoping that would get her an extra snack later on. Whatever the case, Honor was thankful for her daughter's quiet cooperation. Sharing a room with Lily could be difficult. Especially when Honor was tired and her daughter was not. Unfortunately, the bungalow only had two bedrooms, and it had seemed more important for Candace to have her own room than for Honor to have one.

Exhausted, Honor dropped onto her bed, kicking off her

rubber-soled shoes and stretching out on top of the quilt. She should get up and change, wash her face, go through her normal before-bed routine, but she was too tired to do anything more than lie there.

A few hours of sleep. That's all she needed.

Then she'd be ready to tackle the chores and the unpacking with the energy and enthusiasm the jobs required. If she worked efficiently, her three days off would be plenty of time to get the house under control and regain the routine she and the girls had thrived on when they were in St. Louis. By the time Honor returned to work on Tuesday, she'd have the last of the moving boxes unpacked, the backyard would be free of debris and the little bungalow she'd rented sight unseen would feel more like home.

FOUR

"Hey! Mister! Hey! Can you hear me?" The muffled voice drifted into Grayson Sinclair's dreams, pulling him toward consciousness. Exactly where he didn't want to be.

He bit back a groan and threw an arm over his eyes, refusing to open them. He'd spent most of the past forty-eight hours catching up on work and calling contractors to try to line up workers who could make his parents' Lynchburg rental property handicap accessible. Jude would be staying there once he was released from the hospital.

It had taken ten phone calls to convince his brother of that. Only by threatening the unthinkable—their mother staying with Jude in his New York apartment while he recovered—had Grayson been able to achieve his goal. He wanted his brother close to family during the long recovery ahead. Eventually his brother might thank him for that.

"Mister?" The little kid's voice intruded again, and this time he couldn't ignore it.

Grayson scowled and dropped his arm, glancing around the sunny solarium, searching for the speaker. He spotted her quickly, the Day-Glo pink coat and bright pink tutu she wore standing out in stark relief against the grays and browns of early winter. Face pressed against the glass, dark hair spilling out in wild ringlets, Honor Malone's daughter looked just as impish as she had two days ago. Not that he'd thought much about the Malone family since then.

Liar.

He'd thought plenty about them. Especially Honor. If he hadn't been so busy, he might have given in to temptation, stepped through the shrubs that separated their property and knocked on the bungalow's door.

"What are you doing out there, Lily?"

"Looking for a horse."

"Well, you're not going to find one here." Grayson strode to the door and pulled it open, the blast of icy cold air nearly stealing his breath.

"Are you sure? Because I was thinking maybe you had one inside your house. It's a big house. Really big enough for a horse to live in." She stared up at him, her eyes a deep shade of blue, her cheeks pink from cold.

"Sorry. I don't keep horses in my house." He grabbed a jacket from one of the fancy coat hooks his ex-fiancée had insisted be installed.

"But Mommy said you had to have one."

"Did she? And did she say you were allowed to come over here to look for it?" He slid on the jacket and put a hand on Lily's shoulder, steering her toward the back of his property as he spoke.

"No."

"Does she even know you're out here?"

"Lily? Lily Mae Malone, you'd better come out from wherever you are. Right now!" Honor's shrill voice carried across the cold backyard and answered Grayson's question.

Obviously, she hadn't known her daughter was outside, and obviously Lily was about to catch some major trouble.

He glanced down at the little girl, almost feeling sorry for her. Almost, but not quite. The world was a dangerous place. A kid like Lily should never be wandering around in it alone.

"She's over here," he called out to Honor. They were still fifty yards from the back edge of his property when the thick shrubs parted and she raced into view, dressed in what looked like red nurse's scrubs. Her straight black hair gleaming in the sunlight, her skin glowing pink from exertion or cold, she ran across the yard and pulled Lily up into her arms.

"Thank goodness you're all right. Candace and I were worried sick. What were you thinking leaving the house by yourself?" The words flew out in quick, frantic pants of breath, fear flashing in her eyes as she met Grayson's gaze.

Green eyes. Much brighter than he'd remembered. Flecked with blue and gold. Rimmed with black lashes that were striking against Honor's creamy skin. For a moment, Grayson felt caught in her gaze, pulled deep into a world he'd stayed away from for months. When he looked in Honor's eyes, he forgot why.

"I'm so sorry, Grayson. I hope Lily wasn't bothering you." Honor's voice shook slightly as she spoke and her arms were tight around her daughter as if she planned to hold the little girl close forever, keeping her safe from the ugliness that existed in the world.

If only life were that simple.

If only a person really could keep a loved one safe by sheer force of will. "She wasn't."

"I'm not sure I believe you. Lily has a one-track mind about certain things. Though I have to say, she's never pulled a stunt like this before." She paused, looking her daughter in the eyes. "And she never will again. Will you, Lily Mae?"

"I just wanted to see if he had a horse, Mommy. A white one. Like you said. Remember?"

Honor's brow furrowed and she frowned. "I remember. Just as I'm sure *you* remember our rules about going outside without permission. Don't you?"

"Yes." Lily lisped the response, her face a mirror of Honor's. Both were pink-cheeked with freckles dotting their noses. Lily's hair was a few shades lighter than her mother's, her eyes blue rather than green, but she possessed the same heart-shaped face and high cheekbones. And the same indefinable quality that would make people want to take a second look.

They made a pretty picture as they frowned into each other's eyes, barely aware of Grayson. If he'd had a camera with him, Grayson would have snapped a picture. It was the kind of moment he'd thought he'd see a lot of as he watched his wife and children blossom in the large house his ex-fiancée, Maria, had insisted on...before she'd informed him that kids weren't in her plans for at least another five years.

He frowned, wondering why he was thinking about something he'd decided months ago to put out of his mind.

"If you knew the rules, then why did you break them? You could have been hurt, or gotten lost. Anything could have happened. We've talked about this before. You know how important it is never to go out alone." Honor's words broke into his thoughts, and he was glad for the distraction.

"I'm sorry, Mommy. I just needed to know." There were tears in Lily's eyes, and Grayson felt his heart melting.

"What did you need to know?"

"If he was a prince. A real one with a white horse.

Because if he is, he can slay the dragon. And then everything will be okay."

"Sweetheart, we've been over this a hundred times before. There are no princes in Lakeview. And there are no dragons, either." Honor spoke with weary resignation, and Grayson wondered how many times and in how many ways she'd said the same thing.

"But, Mommy—"

"Lily, enough! Just for a while, let's stop talking about it." Honor brushed a hand over Lily's cheek, shivering a little as she set her daughter on the ground. The nurse's scrubs she wore were short sleeved and her feet were bare. She must have run from the house without thinking of anything but finding Lily. That kind of desperation, that kind of fear was something Grayson understood only too well. When he'd received the call about Jude, he'd left the house unlocked, left the lights blazing, left cases that were going to trial. He'd driven to New York with nothing but his wallet and the clothes he was wearing. And he'd stayed there until his brother was on his way to recovery.

"Here." He shrugged out of his jacket and dropped it around Honor's shoulders. For a moment she met his eyes again, the worry and fear in her gaze making him want to tell her that everything would be okay. That her imaginative little girl would stay safe. That the world would be as kind to Lily as it should be.

Then she looked away, the contact between them gone, the moment spent. "Thank you, but now you'll be cold."

"I'm wearing a sweater. I'll be warm enough."

"My mother would call you a true gentleman."

"Yeah? And what would you call me?"

She eyed him carefully, her gaze touching hair he knew needed a trim, the beard that he hadn't taken time to shave, the thick sweater his sister Piper had bought at a county craft fair a few months ago and given to him because, she'd said, it matched his eyes. "Trouble."

Her answer surprised him, and Grayson laughed. The first honest-to-goodness laugh he'd had in weeks. Maybe longer. "I guess you get points for honesty."

"And I guess you get points for not denying the truth." Honor took her daughter's hand. "We've got to get back home, Lily Mae, or Candace will have the police out here looking for you."

"But, what about the dragon? We need to find a prince to slay him before he gets us."

"There is no dragon, so there's no way he could get us."

Really, Grayson should stay out of it. Go back inside the house, close the door and let Honor and her daughter work things out without an audience. Unfortunately, staying out of things wasn't something Grayson had ever been good at. "Listen, Lily, I don't have a white horse. I don't have a horse at all, but if a dragon does show up, I'll do my best to slay it. I promise."

Honor stiffened, shooting Grayson a censorious look. "Promises are a dime a dozen, Grayson. As easily broken as they are made. Besides, there *are no dragons*. And if there were, I would figure out a way to slay them myself." Obviously, he'd touched on a sore point, but Grayson didn't plan to apologize.

"I'm sure you would, but a little help wouldn't be amiss in a situation like that."

"Besides, Mommy, the princess never slays the dragon. Only a prince can do that." Lily had broken away from her mother and was spinning around in circles, her tutu as bright as the flowers that had bloomed last spring.

"Who says princesses never slay dragons?" Honor continued walking across the yard, Grayson's coat falling past her thighs. She looked smaller than he'd remembered. More delicate.

"All the books, Mommy. Every single one."

"And we know how true those books are, don't we?" There was amusement in her words and in the fond gaze she settled on her daughter.

"They are true. They really are."

"Oh, Lily, what am I going to do with you?" Honor spoke so quietly, Grayson almost didn't hear.

"You're going to keep doing what you've been doing—loving her unconditionally." He bent close to whisper the words in Honor's ear and caught the heady aroma of summer sunshine and wild flowers.

"You're right. That's exactly what I'll do. That, and worry every day that her dreams will take her away from me." She smiled, but the sadness behind her eyes was unmistakable. "For now, I'm just enjoying her. She's such a funny little girl."

"And a special one."

"That, too." Honor called to Lily and pushed through the heavy shrubs.

Grayson knew he should probably stay on his side of the barrier, but knowing that didn't stop him.

He followed the two Malones through the shrubs and into Honor's backyard, pausing as the two went up the back steps, not sure how he'd even ended up there. Honor was pretty. Intelligent. Compassionate. He'd known other women like her. What was it about Honor that made him want to know more?

That made him want to talk to her about everything and about nothing?

She turned before she opened the door, the morning sunlight reflected in her blue-black hair and shimmering in her forest-green eyes. The sight made the breath catch in Grayson's throat, made his heart leap in acknowledgment of her simple beauty.

"I'm putting on a pot of coffee if you'd like a cup."

Being pulled into Honor and Lily's lives probably wasn't the best idea. Then again, sharing a pot of coffee with a neighbor seemed a lot more appealing than reading the deposition he'd left sitting on the table in the solarium. And, quite honestly, he wasn't ready to say goodbye yet. "That would be great. Thanks."

"Come in then, but just remember, I've been working long shifts. The house is still a bit cluttered."

"Why would I notice clutter when I have two beautiful ladies nearby?"

Lily must have been listening, because she giggled.

Honor, on the other hand, didn't look amused. "There you go again with your flattery."

"Is it flattery when it's the truth?"

"Grayson Sinclair, you are more trouble than I have time to deal with." Honor shook her head and pushed open the back door, ushering Lily into the house. "Come in anyway. We'll discuss what flattery is after I start a pot of coffee. And Lily, we'll discuss the consequences of your behavior after Mr. Sinclair leaves. Off to your room, now."

"But, Mommy—"

"Lily Mae, is that you I hear?" Candace's voice rang out from the kitchen, cutting off whatever argument Lily might have made. Too bad. The kid was a good negotiator. A lawyer in the making. And Grayson enjoyed seeing her in action.

"Yes."

"Where have you been? Do you realize how worried I've been? I was just getting ready to call the police."

"I'm sorry, Aunt Candy."

"Sorry? Sorry doesn't help. You should never have disobeyed me. Do you realize…" Candace's voice trailed off as she stepped into the mudroom and saw Grayson. "Oh, sorry. I didn't realize we had company."

"Mr. Sinclair is here for a cup of coffee. It's a thank-you for keeping Lily safe until I found her."

Honor seemed to want to qualify the invitation. Grayson told himself that that was fine with him. Whatever it was about her that attracted him, he didn't have time to act on it. He had work to catch up on, a brother to worry about. He didn't need to add more complications to his already complicated life.

Whether or not he wanted to, that was a different story altogether.

"You were in the neighbor's yard? Lily, how could you?" Candace brushed thick blond bangs from her eyes and sighed, taking the little girl's hand and leading her from the room. Lily sent a beseeching look in Grayson's direction, and he did his best not to smile at the dramatics. Honor had quite a kid.

"She's quite a drama queen, my daughter." Honor spoke as she started the coffee maker, her voice lilting and exotic.

Maybe it was the accent Grayson found so appealing.

Or maybe it was simply the woman herself. "She's definitely got an acting career ahead of her if she wants one."

"Funny you should say that. Her father always dreamed of

being a film star." Honor smiled, but it didn't hide the sadness in her eyes.

"And did you always dream about being a nurse?"

"I always dreamed about being married and having kids."

"Then I guess you achieved your dream."

"I guess. Sometimes, though, the reality of a dream isn't nearly as beautiful as the dream itself." She poured coffee and offered him a cup, her expression filled with a yearning that made Grayson's chest tighten.

"You didn't have a happy marriage."

"Everyone's definition of happy is different, Grayson. I was content enough. How about you? Did you always want to be a prosecutor?"

"For as long as I can remember."

"Then you've achieved your dream, as well."

"Yes, but it's like you said. Sometimes the reality doesn't quite live up to the dream."

"You're not happy?"

"I'm happy." But he wasn't content. And until this minute, standing in Honor's warm kitchen, sipping coffee and listening to the lyrical sound of her voice, he hadn't realized it.

"Then you've got nothing to complain about." She reached into the cupboard and pulled out the box of cookies she'd offered the previous day. "Biscuit?"

"Thanks." He took one, watching Honor's face as she bit into one of the rich shortbread rounds. "I'll have to remember how much you love these cookies if I ever visit Ireland."

"No worries. Mum keeps me well stocked."

"Yes, but I'd still want to bring back a gift for a friend."

"Is that what we're going to be, Grayson?"

"Maybe."

"Unless my daughter comes in your yard and bothers you again?" She grinned, all the sadness and longing that had been so clear in her face gone.

"Actually, I was thinking we would become friends unless we became something more than that." The words slipped out, surprising him.

Honor froze at his words, her expression closing off, her bright gaze dimming. "I'm afraid that is an impossibility."

"I don't believe in impossibilities." He set his cup in the sink, took another cookie from the box. Honor might think that a relationship between them was out the question, but he didn't have to agree.

"And I don't believe in more than friendship."

"Then for now, I guess friendship will be enough."

"For now?" The wariness in her eyes was unmistakable, and Grayson wondered what her marriage had been like. Obviously much more disappointing than she'd let on.

"You never know what time will do. It can fade memories and it can change minds. I've got to run. I'm meeting contractors in Lynchburg. We've got to have my parents' rental property ready when my brother is finally released from the hospital."

He purposely shifted the conversation, and Honor seemed relieved. Her shoulders relaxed as she walked him to the back door. "Let me know if I can help your brother in any way."

"I will."

"Thanks again for looking after Lily when she wandered away. Goodbye, Grayson." The way she said it, Grayson was certain she'd meant it to sound permanent.

Too bad.

Because suddenly Grayson's decision to avoid relationships seemed premature. Suddenly the idea of getting to know a woman, of courting her, of inviting her into his life seemed much more appealing than it had a few hours ago.

FIVE

Obviously, Honor was even more tired than she'd thought. Why else would she have invited Grayson Sinclair in for coffee? There were unpacked boxes awaiting her attention, dishes piled up in the sink and a load of laundry in a basket on the coffee table waiting to be folded. She had more than enough to do without adding entertaining a neighbor.

And not just any neighbor.

Grayson Sinclair.

Handsome, charming, Grayson Sinclair.

She shook her head and drained the last dregs of coffee from her cup, hoping the caffeine would work its way into her system and clear her thinking. The shock of being woken up from a sound sleep and told that her daughter was missing must have scrambled her brains and affected her judgment.

Grayson wasn't all that handsome or charming.

Okay. He was. But that didn't mean Honor found him attractive. She'd learned her lesson about men like that when she'd married Jay. They could be loved, but they couldn't be counted on and they couldn't be trusted. She'd do well to keep that in mind.

Honor sighed, rinsing her cup, and then walked down the

hall. She needed to put Grayson out of her mind and deal with her daughter. She had to make it very clear that there would be no more wandering outside without supervision.

A quick, hard rap on the front door made Honor jump. She turned toward the sound, her heart racing in her chest. The neighbors had stopped by on moving day, but since then there had been no unexpected visitors. Unless she counted Grayson.

She frowned.

There he was again.

Right in the center of her thoughts.

The visitor knocked again, the sound echoing through the cozy living room. Honor knew she shouldn't feel alarmed. There was nothing frightening about someone knocking on the door during daylight hours, but adrenaline coursed through her as she approached the door, telling her she should run and hide rather than see who it was. "Who is it?"

"Flower delivery for Honor Malone." The speaker was female, and Honor relaxed.

Surprised, she peered out the peephole in the door to see a bouquet of blood-red roses.

"Who are they from?"

"I don't know. There's a card though. Want me to open it?"

"No. That's okay. Thanks." She pulled the door open and accepted the flowers from a fresh-faced blonde who looked to be about Candace's age.

"They're beautiful."

"Yeah, they are. Enjoy them. Have a good day." Before Honor could ask any more questions, the young lady hurried back to the driveway, climbed into a bright pink delivery van with the name "Blooming Baskets" emblazoned on the side and drove away.

Honor carried the roses into the house, touching a smooth petal as she set the vase on the coffee table in the living room. Someone had sent her roses.

How long had it been since that had last happened?

Five years ago. She could remember it as vividly as if it were yesterday. Jay had been deployed to Iraq the previous month and Honor had realized she was pregnant soon after. She'd called him with the news and a day later he'd managed to have four dozen roses delivered to the apartment. One dozen for each member of their family. Four dozen more than they could afford on his soldier salary.

Honor blinked away the memory, reaching for the note attached to the vase.

I've missed you.

Three words that meant absolutely nothing to Honor. She turned the card over, searching for a name, but there wasn't one. No signature. Nothing indicating who had sent the flowers.

Curious and slightly uneasy, Honor grabbed the phone and called information, then dialed the number of the florist. The owner tried to be helpful, but the information she had was vague. A dark-haired man wearing a suit had ordered the flowers. He'd paid cash and hadn't given a name.

Honor found the news oddly disturbing.

She touched a petal again, frowning as she stared down at the flowers.

I've missed you?

She didn't know anyone in Lakeview well enough to be missed by them, and she couldn't believe someone from St. Louis had come all the way to Lakeview to send her a bouquet. If someone in the city had missed her enough to come to town, surely he would have stopped in to visit before going home.

"Oh, flowers!" Candace walked into the room, her eyes bright with excitement as she caught sight of the roses. "They're gorgeous."

"They are, aren't they?"

"So why do you sound less than happy about getting them?" As usual, Candace picked up on Honor's worry.

"I'm just not sure who sent them."

"Is there a card?"

"Yes, but no name." As she spoke, she slid the card into her pocket. There was no sense in sharing her worry with Candace.

"If you really want to know who sent them—"

"I already called the florist. They weren't able to tell me who the flowers are from."

"Of course you called the florist." Candace smiled and shook her head, her sleek ponytail sliding over her shoulder.

"What is that supposed to mean?"

"It means, you don't have an impractical bone in your body. Everything has got to be planned out and scheduled and perfectly in line. Unless it is, you just can't enjoy yourself."

"And is it so wrong to want things to go smoothly?" Stung by her sister-in-law's assessment, Honor turned and grabbed a box from the floor, pulling out a few framed photographs that were wrapped in brown paper and setting them on the end table.

"No, but sometimes it's okay to not have all the answers. Sometimes it's good to just go with the flow."

"'Going with the flow' often means being dragged by a current carrying you where you don't want to go." Jay had been a prime example of that. His laid-back attitude had resulted in more trouble than Honor cared to remember. Unpaid bills, missed appointments, paychecks spent before they ever made it to the bank. That had been Jay's life. It would never again be Honor's.

"Probably, but in this case, it just means accepting a gift from a secret admirer. A secret admirer! How cool is that?"

Not cool, creepy, but Honor decided not to say that to Candace. "Really cool. Is Lily still in her room?"

"She was sitting on her bed looking dejected when I checked on her." Candace didn't seem to care that Honor had changed the subject. Her gaze was on the flowers, a soft smile playing at her lips. Did she dream of finding a handsome prince to carry her away? In all the years she'd been living with Honor, Candace had never mentioned wanting to date, get married or have children.

And Honor knew better than to ask. Candace was as close-mouthed about her dreams as Jay had been verbal. "I guess I'd better go deal with our little escape artist."

"I'll put the flowers on the dining room table. They'll look nice there."

For some reason, the thought of having the flowers sitting in the middle of the table while she enjoyed a meal with the girls didn't sit well with Honor. "No. Just leave them here. They're too pretty to put in the dining room. We'll keep them out here where visitors can see them."

Candace looked doubtful, but shrugged. "If we had any visitors that would make sense."

"We've had a few visitors recently."

"A sheriff and our neighbor." Candace paused. "You know, maybe that's who sent the flowers."

"Who?" Honor headed toward her bedroom, anxious to put the conversation behind her, but not wanting to cut Candace off. Despite her harsh upbringing, Candace was a sensitive soul. Sometimes too sensitive.

"Grayson Sinclair."

"You're kidding, right?" Honor laughed at the thought of her good-looking neighbor sending flowers and a note that said he missed her. Sure, he'd hinted that he might like to pursue something with her. Friendship. More. But Honor knew enough about men like him to know his words were as meaningless as thunder in the desert.

"Why not? He's handsome, rich and has a house to die for."

"If I were looking for someone to date, which I'm not, those wouldn't be the most important qualities on my list."

"Then what would?"

"I don't know. I've not spent much time thinking about it."

"Maybe you should, Honor."

"No. I shouldn't. Now, I'm going to deal with our Lily before she completely forgets she's in her room because she's in trouble."

"And I'm going out. I'm meeting a few friends in town."

"Friends from college?"

"Yeah. A couple of kids from my English class. We're going to study together, then they're going to bring me to the mall in Lynchburg. I'll be home for dinner."

"Have fun."

"I will." Candace walked back down the hall, and Honor pushed open the bedroom door. It was time to deal with Lily. After that, she'd tackle the chores. What she wouldn't do was spend one more minute thinking about the roses or wondering who sent them. Nor would she think about Grayson and his blue eyes that reminded her so much of home. God was in control.

Of her life. Of her daughter. Of Candace. There was no reason to worry and fret. No reason to think beyond this moment.

The future would come soon enough, bringing whatever the Lord had in store. For now, Honor had a house to organize and a child to discipline. That was quite enough for one day.

SIX

The hard day's work had paid off, and by midnight Honor had finished turning chaos into order. Every box was unpacked and ready to be recycled, all the laundry was washed, dried and put away and the dishes were sitting in cupboards, scrubbed free of grime and grease. All in all, it was a good effort toward turning the ramshackle little bungalow into something more. Something worthy of creating memories.

Considering the fact that Honor had signed the rental paper work before she'd ever stepped foot in the house, she couldn't complain. Renting to own had always been her goal, and Mr. Silverton had been as anxious to find someone willing to take on the run-down place as Honor had been to plant roots. If she stayed long enough, she'd own the little bungalow and the half acre of land it sat on. Close to the lake, in a quiet community set apart from the more commercial areas around Smith Mountain Lake, the 1920s-style house had the potential to be a forever kind of place. After years of apartment living, that had appealed to Honor as much as the price. She made decent money as a nurse, but had taken a pay cut to be closer to Candace. The fact that she'd spent the past several years paying off the debt Jay had accrued, hadn't helped

Honor's financial situation. There had been no money for a down payment on a house, no way to come up with closing costs. She'd been sure she'd have to rent an apartment in Lakeview and had been on-line comparing places when she'd spotted Mr. Silverton's lonely little house. She'd known immediately that she and the girls would fit there perfectly.

She glanced around the living room, satisfied with the time-nicked but gleaming hardwood floor, the newly polished art deco mantel. Next weekend, she'd buy paint and put some color on the walls. Maybe a creamy yellow or cool sage. In the meantime, she'd simply enjoy the fact that the place was clean and neat and organized.

Not that everything *had* to be organized for Honor to be happy.

She frowned, thinking over her earlier conversation with Candace and wanting to deny the truth of her sister-in-law's words. Honor was open to a little spontaneity in life. She wasn't completely sold on plans and structure.

Of course she was.

Since Jay had been killed by a roadside bomb in Iraq, she'd kept a tight rein on her little world. Her daughter might not have a father, her sister-in-law might not have a brother, but they would have security. There was nothing to be ashamed of in wanting that for her girls, was there?

No. Of course there wasn't.

And liking things orderly and predictable did not make a person boring.

She circled the room, checking the windows and the front door to make sure they were locked. She studiously avoided looking at the roses. They'd been sitting on the coffee table all day, and if it wasn't for the fact that the girls would demand an explanation, she probably would have given the flowers a new home in the trash can outside.

Blood-red roses from someone who missed her.

She shuddered, turning off the light and leaving the room. Everything was locked up tight. The girls were safe in their beds. Still, she couldn't shake the unease that shivered along her spine as she changed into thick flannel pajamas.

The wood floor was cold under her feet, the house silent as she crossed the room and stood over her daughter's bed. Lily slept soundly, her face turned toward the wall, a stuffed bear clutched in her arms. Even in sleep she looked restless, her brow furrowed with whatever images filled her dreams, her body tense as if she were ready to leap from the bed.

"Lily-girl, you're going to be the kind to put gray hair on your mother's head, aren't you?" Honor whispered as she brushed strands of baby-fine hair from Lily's cheek. "It'll be worth it, though, to see you grow into the woman God plans for you to be."

She let her hand drop away from her daughter's cheek, and moved to the window that looked out over the backyard. In St. Louis, they'd lived on the third floor of an apartment building in a decent part of the city. There'd been no worry that someone might knock out a pane of glass and get inside. Now that they lived in a one-story house, Honor realized just how little protection a window offered. A brick could easily shatter the glass. Then, as quick as a wink, danger could enter their sanctuary.

She scowled, leaning her head against the cold glass and staring into the darkness. At times like this, she missed Jay desperately. Despite all the disappointments and heartache he'd caused, his solid presence had always made Honor feel safe. Alone with the girls, she felt vulnerable. It was a feeling she didn't like at all.

Darkness pressed against the glass, the shadowy world beyond the window cast in shades of black and gray. Honor had never been afraid of the dark, but suddenly she was sure a million eyes were watching her from the gloom.

What she needed to do was climb into bed, close her eyes and sleep. When the sun rose, she'd feel more herself and less—

A face appeared at the window. Pale against the darkness. Hollow eyes. Blurred features.

A mask?

Honor screamed, stumbling back, her heart slamming against her ribs, her body cold with horror. She grabbed the phone, lifted Lily and raced from the room, sure that at any moment she'd hear the sound of shattering glass.

Call 911. Get the police here.

Frantic, she dialed the number as she skidded into Candace's room, praying the Lakeview police would arrive before whoever was standing outside her window realized just how easy it would be to get inside the house.

Something was going on at Honor's house. Grayson watched with mounting concern as the formerly dark bungalow lit up one room at a time. There were plenty of reasons he could think of for Honor to be walking through her house flipping on lights, but none of them were good. The one that was the most worrisome involved Lily wandering outside again.

Grayson rubbed the back of his neck and watched as the outside light beside Honor's back door went on. Midnight wasn't the best time to be awake, but since he and his neighbor both were, maybe he should take a quick walk across the yard and find out exactly why every light in Honor's house was blazing.

In a matter of moments, he was stepping out his back door and starting across the yard. Still and silent, the night seemed hushed with anticipation, the sky deep azure and speckled with stars. Nothing moved. Dry grass crackled beneath Grayson's feet, the thick scent of pine needles and wood smoke wafting on the frigid air.

Somewhere in the distance a siren blared, the sound a discordant note that jarred Grayson's nerves and made the hair on the back of his neck stand on end. Lakeview was a quiet town not given to sirens in the middle of the night. Something was going on, and he prayed it wasn't what he'd first suspected. It was too cold for a little girl like Lily to be outside. Too dark. Too dangerous. Sure, Lakeview was safe, but no matter how safe a neighborhood was there were always predators just waiting for an opportunity to strike.

He pushed through the shrubs that separated his yard from Honor's and hurried to the back door. Despite the bright lights, the bungalow was silent, the windows empty of life. Grayson could see into the kitchen, but none of the Malones were there. He knocked on the door, anxious to make sure Lily was okay. The kid had a wild imagination and the kind of gumption that could get her into all kinds of trouble.

It would kill Honor if anything happened to her little girl. Images flashed through Grayson's mind. Family members sitting in the courtroom, listening as the criminals who had stolen their loved ones were tried. So many tears. So much heartache. It was what drove Grayson to continue as a prosecutor, and what drove him now. If Lily had wandered away, they needed to call in tracking dogs, gather the teams who would make finding her a possibility.

Grayson knocked on the door again. This time with more force.

"Who is it?" Honor's voice was thick with fear.

"Grayson."

"It's late for a visit, isn't it?" She didn't open the door, and Grayson didn't ask her to. Whatever was going on had frightened her enough to make her hesitant. That was good. Smart. As far as he was concerned, a little caution went a long way toward keeping people safe.

"I saw all the lights on, and I wanted to make sure everything was okay."

"We're fine. Thank you."

"Lily hasn't escaped again?"

"No."

"So she's with you?" Grayson knew there was a problem. Whether it was big or small remained to be seen, but he did intend to find out what it was.

"Yes, where else would she be?"

"Looking for horses and princes?"

"Not this time."

"Then I guess there's another reason that all the lights in your house are on?"

"We've had…" She paused as if trying to decide what to say. "An incident."

"What kind of incident?" The sirens were screaming closer, the throbbing pulse of them pounding in Grayson's ears.

"The kind that requires police help." The door cracked open, and Honor peeked out, her face pale, silky strands of hair falling across her cheeks. Just seeing her made Grayson's heart trip and his pulse race. It was as if he'd been waiting his entire life to meet her and as if he had known her forever.

"Do you want me to wait while you speak to the police?"

She hesitated, and Grayson was sure she was torn between needing another adult around and wanting to take care of her family herself.

Finally, she pulled the door open farther, her gaze darting to the yard behind him. "You didn't see anyone out there, did you?"

"No."

"Good. Maybe that means he's long gone."

"Who? What happened, Honor?" He put his hands on her shoulders, looking down into her face and trying to will some of his calmness into her trembling body.

"Someone was at the window staring in at me. I only saw him for a second, but it was enough." She shuddered, turning as a loud knock echoed through the house. "That must be the police."

He followed her through the kitchen and dining room and into the living room. A bouquet of roses sat on the coffee table, blood-red and velvety. A gift from a friend? An admirer?

Honor fumbled with the chain that hung across the front door, her hands shaking so hard she couldn't seem to maneuver it open.

"Let me help." Grayson covered her hand with his, sliding the chain off in one easy movement. For a moment, he let his palm rest against her knuckles, letting the warmth of his skin heat the coolness of hers. Then he let his hand drop away, gently nudging her aside so that he could open the door.

Sheriff Reed stood on the other side of it, a scowl darkening his face as he met Grayson's eyes. "I hear there's been some trouble out here."

"So Honor was saying."

"You were here when the incident occurred?"

"No. I came over when I saw all the lights being turned on. I wanted to make sure everything was okay."

"But you didn't see anything?"

"I'm afraid not."

"According to the dispatcher, someone was looking in your window." Jake addressed the comment to Honor, his gaze searching the room as if a clue as to what had happened might be there.

"Yes, the bedroom window."

"It looks out over the backyard?"

"Yes."

"Why don't you show me which one?"

"The bedroom is right this way." Honor led Jake down the hall, and Grayson stayed put, walking to the windows and checking the locks on each. They were old. Not much protection if someone wanted to break in. He needed to replace them. Make sure that no one could harm Honor or her girls.

But would she let him? Honor seemed so determined to do everything herself—and to keep him at a distance. Grayson had a feeling that if he insisted on stepping in, she'd push him away completely. Better to step back than risk that.

If Honor wanted help, he'd give it, but forcing his ideas on a woman who'd obviously had her fill of men, a woman he was determined to get to know better, wasn't a good idea.

He'd find another way to make sure she was safe. Maybe a few subtle hints about the condition of her window and door locks?

It only took a few minutes for Honor and Jake to return, but it seemed like a lifetime.

He walked toward them as they reentered the room. "What did you find?"

"Nothing yet. I'm going outside to look around." Jake started toward the kitchen, and Grayson followed.

"I'll come with you. Two people looking will make finding something more likely."

"You know better than that, Grayson. If there's evidence out there, I don't want it contaminated. I'll be back in a few minutes." Jake walked outside, and Grayson stared after him, frustrated and not sure why. Jake was right. Of course he was. But Grayson wanted to be out there with him, searching for the guy who'd frightened Honor so badly.

"Come back in the kitchen. I'll make some coffee." Honor touched his bicep, her fingers barely grazing his arm before dropping away. Even that was enough to send Grayson's pulse racing.

"I'd rather be out there with Jake."

"I can see that. You look like you're ready to knock someone's head off."

"And you look ready to collapse from exhaustion." He studied her face, wondering if the dark circles beneath her eyes had been there earlier in the day. Raising a child alone had to be a challenge. No matter how much you loved her. And then to have this would-be intruder? No wonder she looked so tired.

"It's been a long day."

"Things will be better tomorrow." He reached out and tucked a strand of hair behind her ear, surprised when she didn't move away.

"Funny, that's what my dad always says when I'm having a tough time."

"It sounds like your dad is a smart man."

"I guess that makes you one, too. I'm sorry you keep getting pulled into my troubles, Grayson."

"I haven't been pulled into anything."

"Yet here you are."

"We're neighbors, Honor. Working our way up to friends." And maybe something more, but Grayson decided Honor would rather not hear that again. "Should I have ignored all the lights going on in your house at midnight?"

"Plenty of other people would have."

"I'm not any of them, Honor. And I won't stand back and watch you deal with this trouble by yourself."

"Maybe that's what I want you to do." She sounded more uncertain than confident, and Grayson took her hand, squeezing it gently.

"It's what you think you should want me to do, but it's not what you want. For tonight, why don't you let that be okay?"

She studied his face for a moment, seeming to take in everything about him. Not just his appearance, but his soul. Finally, she nodded and squeezed his hand. "Okay. Just for tonight."

"For tonight."

When she pulled away from his hold, he let her, following as she leaned out the open mudroom door.

"Do you think the sheriff has found anything?" Her voice was calm, her words free of the anxiety he'd seen in her eyes.

"If he has, he'll let us know."

"Hopefully it will be soon. The girls are scared, and I want to be able to tell them everything will be okay."

"And who will tell you that, Honor?"

She glanced over her shoulder, meeting his eyes, her expression guarded. "I'm an adult. I don't need anyone to. I hear the sheriff coming back. Hopefully he has some news." She stepped out in the cold, cutting off their conversation.

Grayson followed, tensing when he saw Jake's grim expression. He'd found something.

SEVEN

"Ms. Malone, can you come with me, please? I have something I'd like to show you."

Honor didn't like the sound of that, but she stepped toward the sheriff anyway, aware of Grayson's gaze as she did so. His intense focus was as warm as a physical caress, tempting her to reach back, take his hand, permit herself to accept the support he'd offered.

Of course she wouldn't.

Not even for tonight.

She'd allow him to be here, allow herself to face whatever the sheriff had found with Grayson by her side, but she wouldn't allow herself to depend on him. That could only lead to heartache.

"What is it?" A dead animal? A bloody note? A *body part?* Something horrible. She was sure of it.

"Nothing terrible. Just something I want your thoughts on."

Okay. So it wasn't a body or a piece of one. At least Honor could take comfort in that. "Where is it?"

"On the slide. I'd like to know if it was there earlier."

"As far as I know, there hasn't been anything left on the slide today." She hurried after him, acutely aware of Grayson following close on her heels. Two days ago, she hadn't known he existed. Now it seemed as if he'd become a fixture in her life.

How that had happened, she didn't know. She only knew it was troubling. And that now wasn't the time to think about it. She needed to focus on the task at hand, find out what the sheriff had found and figure out how she was going to deal with it.

Up ahead, the sheriff had stopped near the old swing set, and Honor hurried to catch up with him, her feet catching in tangled weeds. She tripped, arms windmilling as she searched for balance. Grayson grabbed her elbow, holding her steady while she regained her footing, his palm warm through the thick flannel of her pajama top, his breath whispering against her cheek as he leaned down to look into her eyes.

"Are you okay?"

"Fine. Thank you."

"Are you sure? You don't have to look at what Jake has found. I can check it out for you, and we can discuss it in the house."

"No. This is my problem. I need to deal with it."

If he'd insisted, she might have been able to pull from his grasp, walk toward the sheriff and let Grayson trail along behind her.

He simply nodded, his expression so filled with understanding that tears burned behind her eyes. Had Jay ever looked at her like that? So intently? So filled with compassion?

Honor couldn't remember.

And for reasons she'd rather not examine, she let Grayson escort her the last few feet to the sheriff.

"What did you want me to see?"

"There." The sheriff aimed his flashlight beam at the slide, and Honor's heart sank when she saw what lay on it. No body parts. No frightening notes. Nothing overtly terrifying. Just a rose. Lying by itself, a single thorn visible on the stem. The light cast long shadows that hid the flower's true color, but Honor knew it was deep blood-red, the petals delicate and velvety. Just like the flowers that were sitting on her coffee table.

Honor took a deep breath, trying to control the terror that thrummed along her nerves. "A rose. How did it get there?"

"I was going to ask you the same thing." Sheriff Reed leaned closer to the slide, but didn't touch the rose.

"I have no idea."

"You do have a vase of roses on your coffee table."

"Yes."

"Is it possible your daughter brought one out here to play with?"

"No. Lily was by my side all day, and we never came outside. A dozen roses were delivered. If we count, I'm sure a dozen will still be in the vase." Her words were sharper than she'd intended, the fear rising inside of her making her stomach churn and her heart race.

"Then apparently the person who was looking in your window left you a gift."

"Not just this one." Honor spoke her fear out loud, sure that the person who'd sent the flowers had been the one looking in the window at her.

"What do you mean?" Grayson's grip tightened on her elbow as he leaned past her to look at the rose.

"The flowers on my table. They were delivered today."

"From?" Sheriff Reed turned to face her, the beam of light jumping away from the rose and landing at Honor's feet.

"I don't know. There was a card, but no name. I called the florist, but the flowers were paid for in cash, and she couldn't tell me the purchaser's name."

"Did you keep the card?"

Had she? Honor remembered shoving it in her pocket when Candace came into the room. Was it still there? "I think so."

"You moved here less than two weeks ago."

It wasn't a question, but Honor answered anyway. "That's right. We moved from St. Louis."

"Was there a reason for that?"

"My sister-in-law is attending Liberty University in Lynchburg. I wanted to be close to her."

"So nothing happened? Nothing that made you feel you had to leave the city?" Sheriff Reed jotted down notes as he spoke, and Honor wondered if he'd noticed her sudden tension.

Grayson must have, because his fingers tightened on her arm, and he looked down into her face. "Something happened. What?"

"A month ago, I was attacked by an intruder in my apartment."

The sheriff stopped writing and looked up from his notebook. "Was it someone you knew?"

"No. He was a drug user, looking for easy cash. I guess he managed to jimmy my lock and get inside the apartment. I surprised him, and he came after me with a knife." Her words came out in a rush, and Honor tried to slow them. "My neighbor was an off-duty police officer. He heard me scream and ran into the apartment with his service weapon."

"What happened to the perpetrator?" Jake was writing again, his hand flying across the page.

"He wouldn't put down the knife. My neighbor had to shoot him." The blood had sprayed everywhere, splattering the walls and ceiling. Honor shuddered at the memory.

"Did he live?"

"No. He died at the scene." She took a deep breath, trying to calm her racing heart. "So, I don't see how it could be related to what's happening here."

"You never know if you'll find connections unless you look. I guarantee I'll be looking." Sheriff Reed tucked the notebook in his pocket. "I'm going to get an evidence bag for the rose. I'll join you inside the house once I'm done. I've got a few more questions I want to ask."

"All right."

"I'm sorry about what happened to you, Honor," Grayson said quietly as the sheriff walked away.

"You don't have to be. I survived. That's more than a lot of people get."

"I know. I've seen what drugs can do. It's never pretty."

"No. It isn't. As frightening as the experience was, I can't help mourning the life that was lost." She glanced at the house. "I'd better get back inside."

"Do you want me to come with you?"

For a moment, she was tempted to say yes. For a heartbeat or two, she wanted desperately to have another adult to lean on. Someone who could take the burden of responsibility—for the situation, for the girls, for their well-being—from her shoulders.

She'd tried that before, though, and all the love that Jay had brought her, all the promises he'd made and dreams he'd shared with her hadn't been able to balance out the promises he'd broken, or the dreams that he'd pursued with more passion than he'd ever pursued Honor.

The thought was sobering, and she shook her head, denying what she wanted in favor of what was safer. "You can go home. Thanks for coming to check on us."

"You know where to find me if you need me, Honor. I'll come. No matter the time or the reason. You know that, right?"

The only thing she knew for sure was that she'd been hurt before, and she didn't want to be hurt again. "I know where to find you if I need you."

His jaw clenched, but he didn't argue, just ran a finger down her cheek, the touch as soft as a baby's breath. "Good night."

He walked away before she could respond.

She knew that was for the best. Grayson Sinclair was a charming and very handsome man. The kind of man she'd do well to avoid having any more contact with.

She had enough problems without adding a man to them. Someone had sent her a dozen roses and had left one on the slide. Had peered in the window at her, his face covered with what could only have been a sheer stocking.

Who? Why?

They were questions she needed answers to, and she could only pray the sheriff would be able to find those answers quickly.

It took less than a half hour for her to realize that the answers wouldn't be forthcoming. She'd tucked Lily back into bed, sent Candace to her room and then answered every question the sheriff issued. In the end, he'd been able to tell her only one thing and it wasn't comforting. According to the sheriff, someone might be stalking Honor. A friend. An acquaintance. A co-worker. A stranger. He'd jotted down names, taken the card that had come with the flowers as evidence, assured her that he'd do everything he could to find the person who'd been looking in her window and then he'd left.

Tired, but unable to sleep, Honor paced the living room, her gaze going to the empty coffee table again and again. She'd asked the sheriff to take the vase and flowers with him even though he hadn't needed them for evidence. Knowing they were still in the house would have kept her awake all night.

She grimaced at the thought. If she didn't stop pacing the living room she *would* be awake all night. A cup of chamomile tea might help her relax.

She stepped into the kitchen, put the teakettle on to boil and stared out the kitchen window into the backyard. Maybe she should be afraid that her Peeping Tom would appear again, but she doubted he'd be back so soon.

What she didn't doubt was that he'd be back.

The phone rang as she pulled a tea bag from the canister, and Honor jumped, her heart crashing against her ribs. Did the stalker have her number? She grabbed the phone, glancing at the caller ID and relaxing as she saw the name. Grayson.

She smiled as she answered, her heart feeling lighter than it had in hours. "Shouldn't you be asleep?"

"Shouldn't you?"

"How did you know I wasn't?"

"I can see the light on in your kitchen. Look outside."

Honor did, and saw a light glowing in one of Grayson's upstairs windows. "I can see yours, too."

"Good. It'll remind you that you're not alone. Now go to sleep. You need your energy to deal with that daughter of yours." The phone clicked and Grayson was gone, but the light in his window continued to glow as Honor sipped her tea, a warm reminder that someone who cared was close by.

EIGHT

Honor was running late the next morning, her frustration only adding to the anxiety that had haunted her dreams and made sleep nearly impossible. Both girls seemed out of sorts, their grumpiness matching Honor's. She liked Sunday mornings to be calm, easy and filled with family time. Not rushed, hectic and filled with grumbling. Honor passed a church called Grace Christian on the way to work every day and had been looking forward to visiting, but in the wake of the morning's frustrations, the idea had lost some of its appeal.

She'd go anyway.

With her parents across the ocean, church family was important to her, and she'd been praying all week that she'd meet people she could grow to care about when she visited Grace Christian.

"Mommy? I want to change into another dress." Lily hovered in the bathroom doorway as Honor put on her makeup. The little girl's eyes were wide and filled with worry, the front of the pink dress she wore clutched in her fists.

"Why is that, sweetie? Did you get something on that one?"

"No, but I need to wear my yellow dress."

"Your yellow dress is a summer dress. You can't wear it when it's so cold outside."

"But it's pretty and cheerful."

"It certainly is, but it's also a sundress. The little strap sleeves on it won't keep your arms warm."

"But I really need to wear it."

"Need to? Why?" This was going to be good. Or bad. Depending on her perspective. Honor decided that after such a difficult night she should try to maintain a sense of humor about whatever Lily said.

"Because it's my only yellow dress."

"Honey, the dress you've got on is beautiful. And pink is your favorite color. I don't see any need to change."

"But, Mommy, I have to change because dragons don't like yellow."

Here they went again. Honor grimaced and tried to hold back her irritation, her sense of humor slipping rapidly. "I thought we decided there were no dragons."

"Just in case there are, we should both wear yellow."

"And who's been telling you that dragons don't like yellow?"

"Aunt Candy. She said if I had a yellow blanket, the dragon wouldn't come into the room. And guess what? I do have a yellow blanket!" Lily's eyes were wide with wonder.

"When did your aunt tell you this?"

"Last night. While you were talking to the police."

"I see." What she saw was that Candace had probably been desperate to get Lily settled back into bed and had said the only thing she thought would get the little girl to sleep. It had worked. Unfortunately, it had caused a whole new set of problems.

"She's right, isn't she, Mommy? Dragons don't like yellow."

"Listen, my darling," Honor pulled Lily into her arms.

"There are no dragons. I keep telling you that, and you know that I would never lie to you, right?"

"Yes."

"Good. So believe me when I say there are no dragons."

"Not even one?"

"No. Not even one. Now, let me finish putting on my makeup or we'll be very late for church."

"Okay, Mommy. But maybe I could wear my yellow ball cap?"

Honor sighed. Obviously, Lily wasn't buying the idea that there were no dragons. More than likely what she really feared was something she couldn't verbalize. The past few weeks had been unsettling and obviously Lily had been affected by them. Honor could only pray that the ones that followed would be better. "Go get my purse, sweetie. There's some ChapStick in there. I think you need to put some on your lips."

"Really?"

"Yes. Hurry, we've got to leave in a minute." The distraction worked, and Lily rushed away. Content. For now. No doubt the conversation would come up again. Honor would just have to keep her cool and continue to reassure her daughter that they were safe. Eventually, Lily would settle down and stop worrying.

In the meantime, Honor would have to talk to Candace and let her know that there were some subjects that shouldn't be entertained in the house. Dragons, for one. Princes, for another. Lily had a big enough imagination without having the adults in her life playing into it.

Honor shook her head and lifted a mascara wand, staring at herself in the mirror as she applied it to her lashes. At thirty, she should still look young and fresh, alive and excited to see what the world had to offer. Instead she looked tired and worn, her dark hair lackluster and lank, her skin pasty, her freckles standing out in stark contrast. She supposed she shouldn't care. After all, she wasn't in the market for a relationship, and what she looked like really didn't matter much to Lily or Candace.

For a moment her mind flashed back to the previous night. To Grayson's bright blue gaze. The way he'd studied her face with such intensity. As if everything about her was fascinating. What had he seen? Surely not the worn mother staring out of the mirror.

Honor frowned. Grayson seemed to be taking up too much of her thoughts. She needed to put him out of her mind, focus on getting her life in order.

"Honor?" Candace appeared at the doorway, dressed in a knee-length skirt and blue sweater, her hair pulled back in a sleek ponytail.

"You look like you're all ready to go. Do you want to drive, or shall I?"

"Actually, I was thinking of driving into Lynchburg and going to church on campus. A lot of my new friends live in the dorms and go to church there."

"That sounds great." Honor hoped her bright tone would hide the disappointment she felt at Candace's words. She knew it was time for her sister-in-law to forge her own path and go her own way, but that didn't make it any easier to watch. Candace had been a scared teenager with pitch-black lipstick and matching hair when she'd stepped into the little house Honor had shared with Jay. It hadn't taken long for the young teen to settle in and settle down. A little love and a lot of understanding had done wonders for the kid whom everyone else had given up on.

And now Candace wasn't a kid, she was an adult with goals and dreams that included Honor in only a peripheral way. The knowledge was bittersweet.

"If you want, I can come to church with you and Lily this week." Candace must have sensed her thoughts. Her eyes were the same deep blue as Lily's, the same as Jay's, but filled with more anxiety than Honor had ever seen in the other two.

"What I want is for you to go and have fun with your friends. Tell me about the church later. Who knows, maybe Lily and I will visit next week."

"Are you sure? Because I really don't mind coming with you."

"Of course, I'm sure."

"Thanks. You're the best." Candace hugged Honor, holding her tight for a moment before she disappeared back in her room and closed the door. Not Honor's daughter or sister, but as much a part of her life as any blood relation could ever be. Honor really would miss her when she finally moved out of the house.

Of course Honor had always known that Candace would eventually grow up and grow away. That was part of life, as natural as heat in the summer and as predictable as the tide. Honor didn't expect or want it to be any different. When the time came for Lily to have a life on her own, Honor hoped she would accept it just as pragmatically. The house would be empty, then. And Honor would be alone.

The thought wasn't comforting, and for the first time since Jay's death, Honor wondered if her decision to stay single was the best one. If maybe finding someone to spend her life with wouldn't be such a bad thing.

She pushed the thought aside, refusing to dwell on it. No matter what the future brought, Honor wouldn't be alone. God was always with her, His presence true and sure. That was enough.

It had to be.

NINE

The phone rang as Grayson was taking a sip of his second cup of coffee. He answered quickly, knowing the only people that would call him early Sunday morning were family. Or Honor.

Had something else happened at the Malone house?

"Hello?"

"Gray? It's Dad."

Grayson tensed at his father's voice, worried that he might be calling with bad news about Jude's progress. "Hey, Dad. Is everything okay?"

"As good as can be expected. The doctors are saying Jude will be here another two weeks at least."

"That's not good news."

"No, but it's better than the alternative."

"Very true. How's Jude taking things?"

"You know your brother. He's fighting everyone and everything."

"Good for him."

"Yeah. As long as he's fighting, I figure he'll be okay."

"Listen, do you guys need me to come back up there? If you do, I'm on my way." As he spoke, his gaze was drawn to the window above his sink. From there he could see the roof of Honor's house. The thought of leaving before Jake caught the person who'd been peeking in her window last night filled Grayson with a sick sense of helplessness. The same way he'd felt when he'd been told about his brother's accident.

"Right now, we need you there more. The rental has got to be ready when Jude is released. We've got a rehab set up in Lynchburg, doctors, everything he'll need."

"I'll keep things moving along here, then. Just keep me posted on his progress." Relieved, Grayson rinsed his coffee cup and put it in the dishwasher.

"I will. Listen, I've got to go. We're heading out to church in a bit. Mom wants to get as many people praying as we can."

"Good idea."

"Yeah. We've already contacted our church in Forest. Make sure you ask your church to pray, too."

"I will, Dad." Though he hadn't actually planned to go to church.

"Thanks, Gray. I'll call you again soon."

Grayson hung up the phone, and ran a hand down his jaw. He'd have to shave if he went to church, and he'd have to dig out his Bible. He frowned at the realization. It had been too long since he'd immersed himself in God's word and too long since he'd taken the time to attend services. A month at least.

Where had the time gone?

His church his father had called it, but even years ago, when Grayson had been attending regularly, it hadn't felt like that. That probably had more to do with Grayson than with the people at Grace Christian. It wasn't that they hadn't tried to make him part of the church family. It was more that he'd been too busy pursuing other goals to participate in the men's

Bible studies, men's breakfasts and the many other activities he'd been invited to.

Guilt reared its ugly head, and Grayson had no choice but to acknowledge it. Church hadn't been important to Maria, and Grayson hadn't pushed the point. During the years they'd dated, he'd gotten out of the habit of regular attendance. Seven months after breaking up with her, he still hadn't gotten back into the routine.

He needed to. He knew it and glanced at the clock, calculating the time it would take him to shower, shave and get ready for church. If he hurried, he might just make it there before the service began.

Grayson pulled into the parking lot of Grace Christian Church with five minutes to spare. Organ music drifted into the corridor and mixed with the sound of happy conversation as he hurried down the hall and pushed open the sanctuary door. The room was packed, most of the pews filled, people talking and laughing as they waited for the service to begin. Grayson searched for his brother Tristan and Tristan's wife, Martha. He didn't see either of them. A few pews near the front looked like they might have room for one more, and Grayson moved toward them, pausing when he caught a glimpse of deep black hair and rosy skin.

Honor.

Her name filled his head and lodged in his heart.

She looked lovely, her hair down and spilling around her shoulders in a silky curtain of black.

She glanced his way as he approached, her eyes widening, her lips turning down in a slight frown. "Grayson. I wasn't expecting to see you today."

"Does that mean you'd rather I not sit with you?"

She was too polite to say yes, and Grayson knew it.

"It just means I'm surprised."

"Why are you surprised?"

"Because you seem like the kind of person who is too busy to bother with church."

Ouch! She'd hit the nail on the head with that one, and Grayson wasn't afraid to admit it. "I've had a lapse in attendance, but realized this morning it was time to come back."

"Because of your brother?"

"Partly, but mostly because of me. There are more important things than work. I think it's past time I started paying attention to them."

She looked up at him, her gaze intense, as if she were weighing the truth of his response.

Finally, she smiled. "You're serious."

"Why wouldn't I be?"

"I thought maybe you had found out I was coming, and decided to do the same." Her cheeks turned pink as she said it, and Grayson laughed softly.

"I had no idea you'd be here. If I had, I would have arrived sooner."

Honor smiled and shook her head. "You're incorrigible."

"I try. So—" he paused and gestured to the pew "—are you going to let me sit?"

Her cheeks grew even redder, and she scooted over, making room for him. The clean fragrant scent of her perfume drifted in the air as he sat beside her. Summery and light, it tugged at Grayson's senses, tempting him to move closer.

He didn't, but only because he thought doing so might send Honor running.

The pastor's sermon on faith during trials touched Grayson's soul, and he prayed fervently during the benediction. For himself and his weakened faith. For his brother's recovery. For Honor. When the last strains of the final hymn faded away, he stepped into the aisle, waiting for Honor and walking out of the sanctuary with her.

"That was a wonderful sermon, wasn't it?" Honor's eyes glowed, and she looked more relaxed than Grayson had ever seen her.

"It was definitely something I needed to hear."

"Me, too. Sometimes it's so hard to understand why things happen. Knowing that God is in control of it all makes it much easier to bear." That she could say that after all she'd been through touched Grayson's heart as few things had. This was real faith. This was true relationship with God. Something alive and vital and real.

"You're a special woman, Honor."

"No more special than anyone else." She brushed a hand over her hair, and he knew his comment had made her uncomfortable. "I need to go get Lily."

"And Candace?"

"She went to a church at the university." Honor smiled, but Grayson couldn't miss the sadness in her eyes.

"You miss having her with you."

"Of course, but she's an adult. It's time for her to step out on her own. Now, I really do have to get Lily. Who knows what kind of trouble she's caused this morning."

She hurried away.

Grayson started to follow her, but was pulled up short by an elderly woman who wanted to discuss suing the county for not maintaining her yard. Grayson spent the next five minutes explaining that it wasn't the county's responsibility, then walked outside.

The air was bitter and cold, whipping against his cheeks and stealing his breath. He could go home and work, but the thought didn't appeal to him. He could drive to Lynchburg and check on the rental property that his brother would be using, but the contractors weren't scheduled to begin work until Monday.

Which left him with plenty to do but no desire to do any of it.

"Mister. Hey, Mister Prince!"

Grayson recognized Lily's voice immediately, and he scanned the parking lot until he spotted her a few yards away.

Dressed in a fluffy pink coat and hat, her cheeks red from the cold, she was pulling against Honor's hold and trying desperately to move toward him.

"Hello, Princess Lily." He smiled and walked toward her, ignoring Honor's uneasy expression.

"I'm not a princess."

"No?"

"Mommy is. And she needs a prince to save her from the dragon."

"I see." He met Honor's eyes, and smiled as she blushed.

"I do not need a prince, young lady. What I need is some Tylenol." Honor shook her head, and tugged Lily toward an old Ford. "This child just does not know when to quit."

"I don't have any Tylenol, but I could offer lunch. That might do just as much to get rid of your headache."

"Headache? I've got an entire body ache." She opened the car door and motioned for Lily to get into her booster.

"Food will help."

"Don't tell me that you actually believe that."

"What I believe is that good food and interesting conversation can solve a multitude of problems."

"I appreciate the offer, Grayson, but I'm not hungry."

"Big breakfast?"

"Mommy didn't eat breakfast." Lily peeked out the open car door.

"Lily, I said to get in your booster." Honor's exasperation was obvious, and Grayson bit back a smile.

"It seems to me that hunger can cause headaches. But you're the nurse. Maybe you've heard something different."

"We're both busy—"

"And we both need to eat." He linked his fingers with hers, tugging her a step closer so that he could see the flecks of gold in her eyes, feel her quick intake of breath.

"Grayson—"

"It's just lunch, Honor."

"Why does it feel like more?"

"Because that's where we're heading. For now, though, it's just a meal between friends."

She hesitated, and he was sure she'd say no. Then she glanced at her daughter, frowning slightly. "It will make Lily's day if we go to lunch with you."

"Then come."

"All right. But I'm taking my own car and I'm paying for my meal and Lily's."

"Taking your own car makes sense. We'll discuss who's paying the bill after we eat."

"We'll discuss it now, or we won't go at all." Her lips were set in a tight line, her eyes flashing.

"You're beautiful when you're irritated, you know that?"

"And you're a man who knows exactly what to say to get what he wants."

"Compliments make you uncomfortable, don't they?"

"I've learned that the sweeter the compliment the more bitter the deception that follows."

"Deception? What kind of men have you been dating?" The question slipped out before Grayson could stop it, and Honor stiffened, reaching into the car to buckle her daughter's straps, then shutting the door before responding.

"I don't date. I don't have time for it. But I was married to a man whose words were sweet cream and warm sunshine. He used them to convince anyone of anything." She spoke quietly, her words devoid of emotion.

"He doesn't sound like a very nice guy." And not the kind of man Grayson thought a woman like Honor would be attracted to.

"Jay was a wonderful guy. Sweet, funny, imaginative."

"And a deceiver."

"Not in his mind. In his mind, he was painting prettier pictures of the way things were and making his life better in the process."

"Deception is deception, regardless of the reasons."

"You don't have to tell me that, Grayson. I know it. And I know the damage it can do." She smiled sadly. "Jay wasn't a bad person. He was just Jay… It looks like my daughter is getting restless. We'd better get to lunch. Where were you planning to eat?"

"Becky's Diner. Do you know it?"

"Know it? We ate there once, and Lily has been begging me to bring her back ever since."

"Then she should be very happy. See you there?"

"Yes." She got into her car, closing the door and pulling away, Lily strapped into her car seat in the back, waving wildly.

Seeing the little girl there, her cheeks still chubby with

baby fat, her eyes wide and filled with happiness, made Grayson's heart clench. Innocence and life wrapped up in a tiny package, Lily was the kind of child who went through life with pure excitement and enthusiasm. The kind of child who could easily be hurt by one of the many predators who wandered through the world looking for victims.

He walked back to his car, more determined then ever to make sure Honor and her family stayed safe.

TEN

Honor hurried Lily across the nearly full parking lot of Becky's Diner, irritated with herself for falling into Grayson's plans. Lunch with him was a bad idea. A really bad one. Yet here she was, doing exactly what she knew she shouldn't.

"Mommy, are you sure Mister Prince is having lunch with us?" Lily bounced next to her, her cheeks glowing pink from the cold.

"Mr. *Sinclair* is having lunch with us. And that is what I would like you to call him."

"I will."

"And no more talk about him being a prince, or slaying dragons or having a horse. Okay?" Honor looked down into Lily's face and tried to force sternness into her voice. Despite the trouble it often caused, Honor loved the quirky side of her daughter's personality. It was so much like Jay's. So much a part of what had attracted Honor to him.

"All right, Mommy."

"And no calling me a princess, either. Because we both know I'm not one. If I were, I'd have ball gowns in my closet instead of work uniforms, and I'd wear glass slippers on my feet instead of sneakers."

"We could get you ball gowns and glass slippers."

"No, we couldn't. But we can get a nice sandwich and a cup of soup for me and something yummy for you."

"Chicken nuggets and fries?"

"Sure." They stepped into the diner and were seated in a booth near the front window of the busy restaurant. From there, Honor had a view of the parking lot and the people walking and driving through it. She imagined Grayson would drive up in something fancy. Maybe a shiny new sports car. A Jaguar. A Corvette. Something showy, like his house.

When a mid-sized charcoal sedan pulled into a parking space, Honor ignored it, turning her attention to the red Corvette that zipped into another space farther away. She was so sure Grayson was going to get out of it, she had to look twice when a short, balding man emerged.

"Look, Mommy. It's Mr. Sinclair." Lily bounced in her seat, poking a chubby finger against the glass.

"Where?"

"Right there. Near the black car."

Honor looked in the direction her daughter was pointing. Sure enough, Grayson was closing the door to the charcoal sedan she'd noticed. "So he is. Now, remember what we talked about, Lil. No going on about your fantasy worlds while Mr. Sinclair is with us."

"I won't." Lily stood up on the bench seat and waved her arms. "Mr. Sinclair, we're over here."

"Lily Malone, you know better than to stand on a chair. And use your inside voice." Honor's cheeks heated as the diner's guests turned to look at Lily.

"Sorry, Mommy." But it was obvious Lily wasn't all that concerned about being chastised. She grinned from ear to ear as Grayson approached, her deep blue eyes shining with excitement. "You finally came."

"We've only been here a couple of minutes, Lily." Honor tried to reel in her daughter's enthusiasm, but she knew it was a lost cause. Life was an adventure to Lily. One that she experienced with pure zeal.

"Is that black car yours, Mr. Sinclair? Because I thought you'd have a special car. Like a gold one. Or a silver one. Or a really fast one." Lily's dark curls were brushing against her cheeks, and despite Honor's reservations about having lunch with Grayson, she couldn't help smiling.

"I used to have a silver car and it was really fast. I traded it in for this one a few months ago." Grayson smiled, and took a menu the waitress was handing him. If he noticed the fact that the platinum blonde was sending him signals about her interest, he didn't show it. His attention seemed to be completely focused on Lily.

"Why did you trade in your car?"

"Because it was too silver and too fast."

"And you got too many tickets while you were driving it?" Honor asked the question before she thought it through, and heat spread along her cheeks. "Sorry. That wasn't a very tactful question."

"There's no need to apologize. I'm known for asking tactless questions. I can't fault other people for doing the same."

"Yes, but asking questions is part of your job."

"Who said I only ask them when I'm doing my job?" Grayson grinned, flashing his dimple, his straight white teeth.

His charm.

That charismatic something that begged Honor to drop her guard and let him in.

She lowered her gaze, staring at the menu and doing her best not to let Grayson see just how much he affected her. Jay had always known how she melted when she looked into his eyes, and he'd used that knowledge to his own benefit too many times. "Our waitress will be back in a minute. We'd better decide what to order."

He didn't respond, and Honor met his eyes. There was curiosity in the depth of his gaze. Interest. Concern. What did he see that made him feel that way? A single mother doing her best to raise a little girl? An overwhelmed widow who hadn't managed to settle into her new life? The victim of a stalker?

"You don't have to worry, Honor. I don't bite." He reached across the table, covering her hand with his, the contact as familiar as it was new.

"I'm sure you don't."

"Then why do you look so scared?"

Because she'd been hurt before. Because she didn't want to be hurt again. "I'm not scared. I'm hungry. Are you ready to order?"

"Sure."

"Without even looking at the menu?"

"There are more interesting things to look at, I think." He smiled again, and Honor's cheeks burned.

"You really are full of flattery, aren't you?" But Honor wasn't flattered. Grayson's words were just a means to an end. Though what end he had in mind, she didn't know.

"Like I've said before, it's not flattery when it's the truth." Grayson glanced at the menu. "What are you two having today?"

Flustered, Honor looked at Lily. "You want chicken nuggets and fries, right?"

"And ketchup."

"Of course, ketchup. Fries aren't any good without it." Grayson said, and smiled at Lily. Honor's heart skipped a beat. There was just something about a man who liked kids.

There was just something about Grayson.

She shoved the thought aside and turned her attention to the waitress who was winding her way back to their table. All Honor needed to do was order, eat and get Lily out of the diner. Then she'd forget that she'd spent an hour sitting beside Grayson at church. She'd forget that his smile made her want to let her guard down. And she'd forget that even with the girls around, her life had become more lonely than she wanted to admit.

She ordered for herself and Lily, doing her best to ignore the way the waitress flirted with Grayson. It seemed to Honor that the woman should be a little more subtle considering that Grayson wasn't at the table alone.

"You're lost in thought," Grayson said as the waitress walked away, an unspoken question hovering behind his words. He wanted to know what she was thinking about, but Honor wasn't willing to share. There was too much on her mind. And too much of that had to do with Grayson.

"I'm just wondering if the sheriff has found anything new regarding those flowers I received." She *had* been wondering that. Just not at the exact moment Grayson had asked.

"You haven't spoken to him?"

"Not since yesterday."

"You could call him now."

"I'm sure if he had something to tell me, he'd have let me know already."

"True, but if talking to him will give you peace of mind..." Grayson shrugged, accepting a refill of water from the overly solicitous waitress.

"The only thing that can do that is finding out who put the rose in my backyard and why."

"Someone wants your attention. It was his way of getting it."

"Who? Why? I keep going back to those two questions, and I keep not finding the answers."

"I can think of a few reasons why off the top of my head." Grayson frowned, then glanced at Lily who was busy coloring on the paper placemat the waitress had given her. "But now is probably not the best time to mention them. As far as who left it, I think it was left by someone in your past. Someone who doesn't want to be forgotten."

"Then he's going to be disappointed, because I already have forgotten him."

"He could be an acquaintance. Someone you've only met briefly. An e-mail contact."

"Or a dragon. A dragon could leave flowers, Mommy. And then maybe he could blow fire on our house." Lily stopped coloring and looked up, her brow furrowed with worry.

"No need to worry about that, Lily. I told you that I'd slay any dragons that came around." Grayson spoke before Honor could, his words firm and filled with conviction. As if he really believed that he could solve whatever problems Honor and her family had.

But without action, words meant nothing. And even if Grayson planned to act on his promise, Honor wasn't sure she wanted him to. She'd been slaying all kinds of dragons on her own for years, even before she lost Jay. Missed mortgage payments, credit collectors, angry people who'd been promised the moon and received nothing. Jay had been as good at breaking promises as he had been at making them.

"Are you okay?" Grayson's voice broke into her thoughts, and Honor blinked, trying to pull herself firmly back into the present.

"Of course." Her tone was brittle. Even she could hear it. Grayson's steady gaze bore into hers, demanding answers she had no intention of giving.

"And yet you're frowning and shredding napkins." He reached across the table, stilling her hands. His fingers caressed her knuckles, soothing tension Honor hadn't even realized she was feeling.

She dropped the napkin, frowning at the small pile of white sitting in front of her.

"I wasn't shredding. I was tearing."

"And that makes it different?"

"It looks like our food is coming. Elbows off the table, Lily." Honor swept the pieces of napkin into her hand, determined to change the subject. She never talked about the problems she'd faced during her marriage. Not with her parents. Not with her friends. And certainly not with men she barely knew.

"Chicken nuggets and fries!" Lily squealed with delight as the preening waitress set a plate in front of her.

Honor did her best to smile at her daughter's enthusiasm. Her stomach was tied in knots, and the thought of eating only made it worse. The sooner she got out of the diner and away from Grayson, the better she'd feel. Talking to him only served to remind her of all the things she used to dream of. All the things she now knew she'd never have.

"Let's say the blessing so we can eat." She linked hands with her daughter and was surprised when Grayson reached across the table to grab Lily's free hand. When his other hand covered hers, Honor couldn't make herself pull away. Couldn't force herself to break the circle of faith that they had formed.

"Would you like me to pray? Or do you want to?"

Grayson's tone was as warm as his palm, his hard face softened by whatever he was thinking.

"You can." Honor's throat was tight with emotions she shouldn't be feeling, and with a longing she didn't want to acknowledge.

"Lord, thank you for the bountiful gifts you've given to us, for this wonderful meal that we can share together, and for the gift of new friendships. Amen."

The prayer was simple and sweet without the frills and showiness of someone who wanted to make an impression. That intrigued Honor, and she looked into Grayson's eyes. Really looked. He didn't glance away. He just met her gaze, letting her search for a truth she didn't expect to find, for sincerity she presumed she wouldn't see, but did.

Honor's pulse jumped in acknowledgment, her heart shuddering with feelings that had died long ago. Feelings that she'd believed were better off dead.

Grayson's eyes darkened, his gaze dropping to Honor's lips, his thumb caressing the back of her hand, and for a moment it was as if Lily weren't sitting at the table chatting about the ketchup she was pouring on her fries. As if there wasn't a restaurant filled with people surrounding them.

Honor's breath caught, her mind went blank and suddenly she couldn't remember all the reasons why she needed to guard her heart. Suddenly the past was nothing but a distant memory, and the present was all that mattered. Grayson's vivid blue eyes, his somber expression, his palm still pressed against her hand. The newness of it all. The simple pleasure of having a man look at her as if she were as beautiful as a flower blooming in the desert.

Shocked, she pulled her hand away and turned her attention to the salad that had been set in front of her. "We'd better eat. I'm sure you have a lot to do this afternoon."

"Nothing that can't wait a while." He didn't smile when he said it, and Honor had the impression that he was as surprised at what had just happened as she was.

She wanted to say something that would change things back to how they'd been before, but the words caught in her throat and she remained silent, picking at lettuce and tomatoes and praying that Lily would eat quickly so they could be on their way.

"Relax, Honor. We're just two friends sharing a meal." Grayson spoke quietly, and Honor nodded her agreement. Anything to avoid discussing what she'd felt.

"Friends sharing a meal?"

"Sure. People do it all the time."

She looked up, got caught in Grayson's smile and found herself returning it and relaxing. He was right, of course. They were having lunch together. It wasn't a big deal unless she made it one. "They do, but *we* won't be if we don't spend a little more time chewing and a little less time chatting. Lily will be done before we even begin."

"Practical as always."

"There's nothing wrong with that."

"You're right. It's a quality I've always admired."

Honor frowned, sure the conversation was heading back into dangerous territory. "Look, Grayson, I think I need to be clear on—"

Her cell phone rang, cutting off Honor's words. She grabbed it, glad for the reprieve. "Hello?"

"Honor? It's Candace." There was a tremor in Candace's voice, and Honor tensed.

"Is everything okay?"

"I don't know. I decided to come home after church so we could all have lunch together."

"I wish I'd known what you'd planned. Lily and I stopped for lunch at the diner." She didn't mention that Grayson was with them.

"It's okay, Honor. No big deal. The thing is, when I got home, there was a package sitting on the porch."

"A package?"

"Yes. It's wrapped in brown paper and has your name on it."

"And this is worrying you?"

"No. Yes. Maybe." Candace's laugh was tight and filled with nervous energy. "I mean, after what happened with that guy in the yard and the flower and everything, the package is just kind of freaking me out. I keep wondering if someone is outside. You know, watching the house. Maybe even watching me. That's silly, I know. And stupid. Just forget I called, okay?"

"I'm not going to do any such thing. How about I just come home and take a look?" Honor glanced at Lily who was dipping a chicken nugget into ketchup. She'd be disappointed to have to leave, but it couldn't be helped. For as long as Candace needed her, Honor planned to be there for her.

"No, really. It's okay. I'm fine. I was just letting my imagination get the better of me—"

"Better to be cautious than to be sorry. I'll be home in about ten minutes." She cut off Candace's protest and hung up the phone, knowing that her sister-in-law must be really scared if she'd called. Asking for help wasn't something the eighteen-year-old liked to do. Honor shoved the phone into her purse and placed a twenty on the table. "I'm sorry, Grayson, but Lily and I need to go home."

"We can't go, Mommy. We're not done eating."

"We're going to have to be done. Candace needs us to come home."

"What's going on?" Grayson stood and threw some money on the table, his brow furrowed with concern.

"Nothing terrible." Honor took Lily's hand and headed for the diner's door.

"But something. Why not tell me what it is? You know I'll just keep asking until you do." Grayson pushed the door open and held it while she and Lily stepped outside.

"Candace found a package on the front porch when she came home. She's a little worried after what happened with the flowers. I told her I'd come home and check things out."

"Did she bring it inside the house with her?"

"I didn't ask."

"Call her and find out. If she hasn't touched it, she needs to leave it where it is. I'll call the sheriff and have him meet you at your place."

"But—"

"Look, I know what you're going to say. 'It's probably nothing. There's no sense in calling the sheriff.' Right?"

"That's kind of what I was hoping *you'd* say."

"There are a lot of things I will do for you, Honor. Lying to make you feel safe isn't one of them. After what happened last night, we've got every reason to be worried about that package."

"That's what I thought, too. I was just hoping that you'd have a different perspective on things."

"Sorry, but my opinion stands. We've got to call Jake."

"Of course, you're right."

"We finally see eye to eye on something." He smiled, but there was no humor in his expression.

"I've got to get home. Candace is waiting."

"Make sure you call her and let her know that the package shouldn't be touched."

"I will."

"Good." Grayson seemed to relax at her words, his warm gaze caressing her face and touching her lips as it had in the diner. Her cheeks heated, and she looked away, unwilling to accept what she was seeing in his eyes.

The kindness. The concern.

The attraction.

She most definitely didn't want to acknowledge that.

There could be nothing between Grayson and Honor.

The sooner she got that into her head, the better off she'd be.

She strapped Lily into her booster seat, got into the car and drove away, telling herself that her racing pulse had more to do with fear than it had to do with Grayson, and knowing she was lying to herself.

ELEVEN

Grayson called Jake before he got in his car, relaying the information and disconnecting as he climbed into the Saturn. He was going over to Honor's, of course. No way did he plan to head home until he knew everything was okay at her house.

He turned the key and started the engine, smiling as he remembered Lily's comments about his vehicle. She'd been expecting something flashy and bold, like the car he'd let Maria talk him into buying two years ago. A silver Jaguar. A smooth ride, but not something Grayson had cared much about one way or another.

He needed something practical, not fancy, and he'd traded in the Jaguar days after saying goodbye to Maria. He didn't regret it. Nor did he regret ending a relationship that had become more a habit than anything else. Maybe if he'd thought about that a little more during the time he and Maria had dated, he wouldn't have asked her to marry him. And maybe if he'd spent more time going to church and reading his Bible and less time pursuing his career, he wouldn't have dated her in the first place.

Looking back, he realized their relationship had been based more on convenience than anything else. He'd wanted marriage. Family. All the things a successful person had. He just hadn't wanted to put much time or effort into building them. Maria had been no different. The fact that neither of them had been brokenhearted when he'd called off the engagement had reaffirmed what it had taken him too long to realize—they weren't meant to spend their lives together.

Until a few days ago, Grayson had been convinced he wasn't meant to spend his life with anyone but himself. Funny how such a short amount of time could change a person's perspective on things.

Funny how willing he was to accept that change.

Now if he could just convince Honor to trust him, things might turn out better than Grayson had ever imagined.

Jake's cruiser was already parked in Honor's driveway as Grayson pulled up in front of her house. He knocked on the front door anyway, waiting impatiently until it cracked open.

"Grayson. Come on in." Honor stepped back, letting him into the living room.

"I see that Jake has already arrived."

"He's in the kitchen."

"Did he open the package?"

"Yes. It seems I've received another anonymous delivery."

"What was it?"

"Come and see." She led him through the dining room, her hair a silky curtain falling straight past her shoulders. No highlights. No forced curls or stiff styling. Just smooth and natural.

He wanted to run his hand over it, let the silky strands slide through his fingers. Instead, he shoved his hands into his pockets and pretended that Honor was any other woman. Or at least, he tried to. "I guess Candace was right to be concerned."

"Yes. Thank you for insisting I call the sheriff. If you

hadn't, I may have convinced myself the package was nothing to worry about and decided not to bother anyone." She glanced over her shoulder as she said it, and Grayson could see the anxiety in her eyes, the tightness around her mouth. Whatever Jake had found was bothering Honor more than she wanted to let on.

"It's never a bother to investigate suspicious activity." Jake spoke as Grayson entered the kitchen behind Honor, but he didn't look up from the box sitting open on the table.

"What's in it?" Grayson stepped forward, his muscles tense, his mind filling with a million possibilities. Years of working as a prosecutor for the state of Virginia had taught him more than he needed to know about the depth of depravity that could live inside a human being.

"Not much, but more than enough to have me worried." Jake reached into the box with a gloved hand and lifted out a piece of paper. "Take a look."

Are you dreaming of me?

The words were black and bold, typed on plain white paper. Generic. Nothing noteworthy about any of it. Still, the message made the hair on the back of Grayson's neck stand on end. How many times had seemingly innocuous things led to dangerous situations? To crime? To death?

"This was with it." Jake lifted a photograph by the corner. It had been taken at night, but Honor's face was clearly visible, her dark hair covered by a knit cap, her coat unbuttoned to reveal what looked like a nurse's uniform. Even in the poor lighting, her skin had a creamy tone, her eyes deep green and filled with worry. Had she sensed the voyeur who'd been watching? Had that been the photographer's goal? To capture her fear and anxiety so that he could replay the moment over and over again?

Anger bubbled up, but Grayson tamped it down again. Getting angry wouldn't help anything. No matter what the crime or who the victim, keeping a cool head went a lot further in making sure the perpetrator was brought to justice. "Do we know when that was taken?"

"Within the last few days. I think after I finished my night shift. I must have been heading to my car. See the building in the background? That's Lakeview Haven." Honor spoke quietly as she pressed in close to Grayson, the subtle scent of flowers and sunshine drifting around her. He knew she only meant to get a better look at the photo, but warmth spread through him at the contact, his heart beating a slow heavy rhythm. The need to protect her, to make sure that the person stalking her didn't ever get close enough to hurt her, made his muscles tighten and his hands fist.

Honor might be strong and determined. She might be independent and capable. But she was no match for evil. No match for the kind of predator that hunted her. "Do you walk to your car by yourself every night?"

"I hadn't had a reason not to." *Until now.* The words were left unsaid, but Grayson heard them clearly enough. They held the kind of fear no person should feel. The insidious kind that left a person awake at night. That made her jump at every creak and groan of floorboards. That left her exposed, vulnerable and helpless.

Grayson had heard the stories over and over again. Each time he'd been filled with anger, but this time was different. This time the victim was a woman he knew. A woman he admired. "Are there people who can walk you to your car?"

"I'm sure someone can." She pressed in closer to his arm, leaning past him to stare down at the picture. Tension radiated from her, and Grayson fought the urge to put an arm around her shoulder, offer comfort that he knew she wouldn't accept.

"If there's no one there who can walk you to your car, call my office. I'll make sure you have an escort. We're not going to take any chances with this. Whoever this guy is, he wants you to know he's around. That means he's getting bold. Boldness can lead to anything." Jake's words were grim. "I'm going to send the box and its contents to the state CSI. They'll be able to search for evidence my team here can't."

"How long will it take for the results to come in?"

"Not long, but sending it out doesn't guarantee we'll be any closer to finding the guy who's doing this." Jake lifted the box and slid it into a large plastic bag. "In the meantime, you need to be careful, Honor. Don't go out alone. Be aware of your surroundings. If you feel nervous about something, don't hesitate to call for help."

"I won't."

"This is a small town. It's hard for a stranger to hide in it. If our guy is someone unfamiliar to people around here, we'll hear about him soon enough." Jake sounded confident, but Grayson wasn't so sure things would play out that way. Stalkers were notorious for staying hidden until they were ready to show themselves.

Their time. Their place. Their agenda.

"Are there security cameras at Lakeview Haven?" Grayson followed Jake as he walked out the front door. "If there are, you might catch a glimpse of our guy."

Jake speared him with a look that said exactly what he thought about being told how to do his job. To his credit he didn't say what he was thinking. "I'm already on it. There are security cameras in the parking area. I'm going over there now to view them."

"I think I'll come along with you and—"

"I don't think so, friend. This is a police investigation. You're a prosecuting attorney. When I have enough evidence to bring someone in, I'll let you know. Until then, it's best if you steer clear and let me do what I've been trained to do." There wasn't any heat to Jake's words, but Grayson felt his own anger flaring up.

"How much information are you going to be willing to share, Jake? Because I want it all. I want to know who's responsible as soon as you do. And I want to know exactly what steps you're taking to bring him in."

"No need to get up in arms about it, Gray. You know I'll keep you and Honor informed." He glanced over Grayson's shoulder, making his point without saying it. Honor was the victim. *She* was the one who needed to be kept abreast of the investigation.

"Thank you for your help, Sheriff Reed." Honor moved past Grayson and stood on the porch steps, her posture stiff as if she hadn't liked the direction of his conversation with Jake. Too bad. Having him concerned and involved might not sit well with her, but Grayson had no intention of backing off.

"I'll be in touch." Jake put the box into the trunk of his cruiser and got into the car, waving before he drove away.

The car was barely out of the driveway before Honor turned on Grayson and said exactly what he knew she'd been thinking. "I appreciate your concern, Grayson, but I can handle the situation. You really don't need to get involved."

"Sorry, but I already am involved."

"Why?"

"Because we're neighbors. Because your daughter seems to think I can protect you. Because I don't want to let her down. And because no matter how much you might want to deny it, there's something between us."

"I'm not denying it. I'm just refusing to allow it."

"Do you think it's that easy? You just decide you're not going to get involved and you don't? Because it's not that easy for me, and I don't think I want it to be." There was heat in his voice, but Grayson didn't care. This wasn't just about friendship. It wasn't just about building a relationship. This was about Honor's safety, and he wouldn't back off until he knew they'd achieved that.

"Maybe that's because you've never known what it's like to have your heart broken again and again and again. Maybe it's because you've never loved someone who loved himself more than he loved you."

"You're right. I haven't."

"Then for you, I can see why stepping into a relationship is easy. For me, it's impossible."

"Nothing is impossible." Grayson took a step closer, inhaling sweet summer and flowers.

"Lots of things are, Grayson." She smiled, the expression filled with sadness. "I put my dreams into someone before. I don't regret it, but I won't do it again. I won't be that vulnerable, that needy. And it wouldn't be fair to let you think I might."

"You don't have to worry about me, Honor. I'm a big boy, and I can take care of myself."

"And you don't have to worry about me. I'm a big girl and can take care of *myself*. I'm going to take precautions until Sheriff Reed finds the person who is stalking me. I'm going to make sure the girls and I are safe."

"Precautions aren't always enough, Honor. I've seen cases like this before. I've tried men who've stalked their prey for weeks, months, even years. Even with the police searching for the person responsible, it can take time to put him behind bars."

"You're not telling me anything I don't know, but what choice do I have but to believe that everything will work out? I've got two girls depending on me, Grayson. My closest family is in Ireland. Even if I could afford to fly there with the girls, I wouldn't pull Candace out of school to do it. Not unless I was absolutely convinced that that was the only way to keep my girls safe."

"What about keeping yourself safe?"

She stiffened at the question. "One thing I've learned is that anything can happen in life. We can live in fear, worrying about the trouble that may be heading our way, or we can trust that God is in control and that anything that happens is part of His plan."

"Everything?"

"Everything. Good and bad."

"You've got a lot of faith, Honor, but faith doesn't preclude caution." Although it helped. Grayson had seen the evidence of it over and over again in his work. Those with strong faith healed more quickly, faced trials with more grace and less anger and were able to move on with their lives in a way that others often couldn't.

"I know that. I also know that when faith is all a person has, she learns that it's enough." She shivered and rubbed her hands up and down her arms. "It's cold. I'd better head back inside."

Grayson knew she wanted him to go.

But for him, walking away wasn't an option.

He cupped her elbow, holding her in place when she would

have walked away. Her bones were delicate beneath his hand, her muscles sinewy and strong beneath her silky dress. "You work nights, don't you?"

"Yes." She didn't try to pull away, but he could feel the tightness of her muscles and the subtle shift of awareness between them. They weren't just two people having a discussion anymore. They were a man and a woman alone together on a porch, chilly winter air urging them closer to each other.

"Can you switch to days?"

"No. Candace is in school during the day. I've got to be here for Lily."

"You could find a day-care provider for a few weeks."

"I looked into it before we came. We can't afford it. Not with Candace's tuition, books, gas for her car." She shrugged. "Besides, the schedule at Lakeview Haven was shifted to accommodate my availability. Even if I could afford day care, I couldn't ask them to rework things again."

"Not even for your own safety?"

"I'll make sure I have an escort." She eased her arm from his, her cheeks flushed with cold, her hair black silk against alabaster skin. It was no wonder Lily imagined her to be a princess. Honor looked like a fairy tale come to life.

"And you'll call Jake if you don't?"

"Of course."

"If you can't reach him, or he can't send someone out for you, give me a ring. I'll make sure you get to your car safely."

"I couldn't ask you to go to all that trouble."

"You haven't asked anything. I'm offering. I've got to make sure I'm around if a dragon shows up and needs slaying. I promised Lily, after all." He smiled, but Honor's expression remained sober.

"I appreciate your concern, Grayson, but we really aren't your responsibility. No matter what promises you made my daughter."

"I guess we have a difference of opinion, then. I don't make promises I don't intend to keep."

She looked like she might argue, but shook her head instead. "I really do need to get back to the girls. Candace has a lot of studying to do, and she'll never get it done with Lily under her feet."

"Take care. Call me if you need anything."

"I'll keep that in mind." She shut the door, the old wood clicking into place with a finality that bothered Grayson more than it should.

What was it about Honor that got under his skin?

She was beautiful, but he'd dated women even more stunning. She had a deep abiding faith that he admired, but he'd known other women who had been just as strong in their beliefs. So what was it about her that made him want to knock on her door, tell her again that he was nearby if anything happened? That made him want to stand on the porch with her in the bitter cold, made him want to think about impossibilities becoming possible? A wife. Children. The kind of family his parents had created.

Whatever it was, Grayson couldn't ignore it and he couldn't walk away from it. Only time would tell if he could convince Honor to feel the same.

The sobering thought followed him into the car and home to the empty house that only seemed emptier since he'd met Honor.

TWELVE

The next two days passed without incident. Honor spent her time at home playing board games with Lily, proofing a paper for Candace, making lists of items she needed to buy at the grocery store. Grayson stopped by twice. Once to borrow a cup of sugar. Once to return the bowl he'd taken with him. Honor didn't believe for a minute he'd needed sugar. She couldn't imagine him baking anything, or needing sugar for his coffee. What had drawn him to her house was the same thing that drew Honor's attention again and again—worry.

Grayson didn't say it. He didn't push for personal conversation, didn't ask to be included in the family's daily life, but Honor knew he wanted to keep close. Make sure she and the girls were okay.

And somehow that knowledge warmed her as she went about her day.

A stalker was watching her, taking pictures of her, biding his time. Waiting for an opportunity to follow through on whatever insane plans he was making. But Grayson was watching, too. And Honor was certain if she needed him, he'd be there for her.

She scowled at her reflection in the mirror, wishing she could turn her thoughts off for a while. She seemed to have

The Editor's "Thank You" Free Gifts Include:

- **Two inspirational suspense books**
- **Two exciting surprise gifts**

YES!

I have placed my Editor's "thank you" Free Gifts seal in the space provided above. Please send me the 2 FREE books and 2 FREE gifts for which I qualify. I understand that I am under no obligation to purchase anything further, as explained on the opposite page.

323 IDL ERWY 123 IDL ESWN

FIRST NAME LAST NAME

ADDRESS

APT.# CITY

STATE/PROV. ZIP/POSTAL CODE

Thank You!

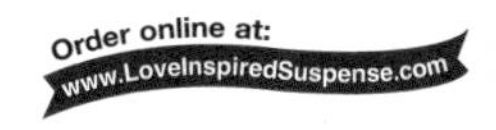

Offer limited to one per household and not valid to current subscribers of Love Inspired® Suspense books. **Your Privacy –** Steeple Hill Books is committed to protecting your privacy. Our Privacy Policy is available online at www.SteepleHill.com or upon request from the Steeple Hill Reader Service. From time to time we make our lists of customers available to reputable third parties who may have a product or service of interest to you. If you would prefer for us not to share your name and address, please check here. ☐

two pet subjects—Grayson and the stalker. The first was pleasant, but worrisome. The second was terrifying. Both were wreaking havoc on her sleep. At night, she tossed and turned, her dreams filled with masked intruders and demonic figures. The lack of sleep showed on her face. The dark circles under her eyes. The pale skin.

She'd thought coming to Lakeview would make life easier for herself and for the girls. Instead, it just seemed to have complicated things. "But I know You're in control of it, Lord. I know that You are going to make sure it all works out okay. I just have to keep believing." She whispered the prayer as she applied the last of her makeup. She had to be at work in twenty minutes, but the thought of leaving the house had her feeling vulnerable and afraid. She had to drive the ten miles to Lakeview Haven alone. Get out of the car alone. Walk to the building. Alone.

"Enough. It's broad daylight. There will be plenty of people in the parking lot. Plenty of people on the porch. You've got nothing to worry about."

"Mommy, who are you talking to?" Lily peeked around the open bathroom door, her blue eyes filled with curiosity.

"Myself."

"Why?"

Why, indeed. Honor crouched down so she was on eye level with her daughter and looked into her eyes. "Because it's better than talking to no one."

"You don't have to talk to no one, Mommy. You can talk to me."

"Very true, my sweet, but you weren't here. I was all alone."

"No you weren't. God was with you. Just like you always tell me. We're never alone."

Out of the mouth of babes.

Honor smiled and hugged Lily close. "I do say that, don't I?"

"Yes."

"Then I guess you're right, and I've got no reason to talk to myself. Now, you be good for Candace tonight, you hear?"

"I will."

"Go to bed on time. No arguing."

"Okay."

"I love you, Lily Mae." She kissed her daughter's cheek, and stepped out of the bathroom. "I'm leaving, Candace."

"Already? I thought you didn't have to be there until two." Candace came to the threshold of her bedroom, her face pale and drawn.

"We've got a mandatory meeting before my shift. I doubt I'll have time to swing back home afterward. I'll probably just stay at the Haven and get some paper work done. I thought I'd mentioned this to you."

"You didn't. I would have remembered." Candace frowned, and Honor's anxiety ratcheted up a notch.

"I'm sorry. I guess with everything that's happened the past few days, I forgot. Do you have plans? If so, I can probably skip the meeting." Though she doubted her supervisor would be happy about it.

"No, that's okay. I don't have any plans. I just was expecting you to be home a while longer."

"Is something wrong? Do you need me to stay? I will. I'm sure my supervisor will understand." She wasn't sure of any such thing, but her family came first, and if Candace needed her home, home was exactly where she would be.

"No. That's okay. I was just surprised." Candace's gaze dropped to Lily, then met Honor's again. "Just make sure you're careful, okay?"

"You know I will be. Call my cell phone if you need me."

"We'll be fine." *Please, please make sure* you *are.*

The words were unspoken, but seemed to shine from Candace's eyes, begging for reassurance. Her parents had shown no interest in her during the past years, and Honor knew that she was all the young woman had.

Honor wanted to pull Candace into a hug, but knew her sister-in-law well enough to refrain. Malones didn't admit to weakness. Jay had told Honor that often enough during their marriage. Candace might not verbalize the sentiment, but from the day she'd entered Honor's life, it had been obvious that was how she felt. Tough, independent, but with a soft spirit that could so easily be bruised and broken.

"I'll be okay, too, Candace." Honor whispered so that Lily couldn't hear, hoping her words would be enough to ease Candace's worry.

"You'd better be." Candace spoke just as quietly, but Honor could still hear the fear in her voice.

Guilt at having to leave followed Honor out the door and into the car. It stayed with her as she drove along the winding road that led out of town. Past pastures steeped in golden sun, across a bridge that spanned a tributary of Smith Mountain Lake, then along the lengthy driveway that led to Lakeview Haven. Guilt that she couldn't do more to make the girls feel secure. Guilt that she'd somehow brought danger into their lives.

"Lord, please help Sheriff Reed find the person stalking me soon. Please keep the girls safe. Keep me safe. Help us to put this behind us and to build wonderful memories here in Lakeview," she prayed. And as she pulled into a parking spot close to the front entrance of the building, a sense of peace filled her.

There was nothing to be afraid of when God was in control. Nothing to worry about. She just needed to cling to her faith, trust that God would work things out according to His will and His way. Everything else would fall into place.

She stepped out of the car and started toward the building, aware of the emptiness of the parking lot and the porch. Obviously, the cold weather was keeping everyone inside. Hopefully it was keeping her stalker inside, too. The thought of him watching as she made her way up the wide steps to the front door made her shiver from something other than freezing temperatures.

"Honor! Wait!" The masculine voice calling from somewhere behind Honor sent her heart tripping. She lunged for the door, pushing it open and racing into the lobby, visions of a masked pursuer filling her mind.

Safe inside, Honor nearly sagged with relief, her heart slowly settling into a normal rhythm. She was halfway across the wide lobby when the door swung open, the sound sending her pulse racing again. She whirled around, expecting to see a stranger highlighted in the afternoon light. Instead, she saw Will walking toward her, his deeply tanned face set in a scowl. "Hey, didn't you hear me calling you?"

"Sorry, it was so cold outside, I couldn't wait to get in where it was warmer."

"Yeah?" His dark gaze raked her from head to toe. "Because the way you were running, anyone would have thought Jack the Ripper was after you."

Jack the Ripper?

Not a good image.

Honor tried to relax and smile. Act like she hadn't been scared out of her wits over nothing. "If Jack the Ripper had been after me, I wouldn't have just been running. I would have been screaming."

"And risk waking Mr. Erickson? I think I'd rather face the Ripper." Will smiled, the irritation in his face easing as they moved toward the nurse's station together.

"True. Mr. Erickson can be a challenge, can't he?"

"A challenge? I got called in this morning because he insisted I stole five dollars in quarters off his dresser."

"You're kidding." No wonder Will looked on edge.

"Do I look like I'm kidding? The old guy asked me to put the change in a sock in the bottom drawer of his dresser. Said he wanted to make sure no stinking thief got his hands on it. Next thing I know, I'm being accused of being a stinking thief." Will nearly spit the words.

"I'm so sorry."

"Yeah. Me, too. Fortunately, this isn't the first time Erickson has pulled something like this. He accused an orderly of stealing his iPod last month. We found that under Erickson's mattress. Once I showed Janice where the quarters were, the matter was dropped."

"It sounds like Mr. Erickson is in desperate need of attention."

"You're probably right about that. I just wish he'd go about getting it in a different way." Will smiled, his gaze searching Honor's. "How about you? Did you have a relaxing weekend?"

"As relaxing as any weekend can be when you've got a four-year-old in the house." That was as much as she planned to say on the matter. Her problems weren't something she wanted her co-workers to know about. Not yet, anyway.

"So, nothing exciting happened? No hot dates or secret assignations?"

Surprised, Honor took a harder look at Will. Was he asking

for a reason other than simple curiosity? Did he know what had happened? Had he somehow heard about the package Honor had received? Or did he know because he'd been the one to deliver it? "No. Why do you ask?"

"Because I'd like to believe you have a more exciting life than I do." Will grinned, flashing straight white teeth.

He was young, brash and too handsome for his own good, but that didn't make him a stalker. Honor really did need to gain control of her imagination. "I'm sorry to tell you, I don't."

"Yeah, well, both of our lives are about to get a little more boring. These meetings tend to drag on. Lots of talk. Little change."

"It can't drag on too long. Our shifts begin in two hours."

"Two hours can feel like an eternity when Janice is talking." Will winked and pushed open the door to the conference room, gesturing for Honor to step in ahead of him.

She did, walking into warmth and soft conversation. The sharp scent of coffee and the sweeter aroma of doughnuts. The easy rhythm of men and women who worked together.

Honor took a seat next a gray-haired RN she'd never met before and introduced herself, relaxing for the first time in what seemed like days. Here, in a room filled with people, she felt safe. Any length of boredom would be worth it for that.

Honor's shift proved to be busy enough to keep her mind off her troubles. Several patients were sick with a flu that seemed to be running rampant through the facility. Another had difficulty breathing and had to be taken by ambulance to a local hospital. Between administering medicine, lending an ear to some of the lonelier residents and making her rounds, she had little time to worry about who might be waiting for her when she left the safety of Lakeview Haven.

By the time she punched out, her back ached and her head throbbed, but at least she wasn't as scared as she'd been when she left home. She waited until Will came to the nurse's station, unwilling to walk out to her car by herself.

"Waiting for me?" He grinned, his boyish charm meant to melt hearts, but doing nothing for Honor. She preferred a little more maturity, a little more experience.

A picture of Grayson Sinclair flashed through her mind, and she shoved it away.

What she preferred was going it alone.

And if she told herself that enough she just might believe it.

"I'm waiting for someone to walk out with."

"Ah, so it's not me specifically you were waiting for. Too bad." His smile faded, but he seemed happy enough to walk to the lobby with her.

"Actually, I *was* waiting specifically for you. We *are* the only two nurses working this shift, after all."

Will laughed and pushed open the door. "That makes me feel so much better."

"What would make *me* feel better is a little warmth." Honor shoved her hands into her coat pockets, wishing she'd brought her gloves to work. Wishing even more that she didn't have to drive home and get out of her car with the night hiding anyone who might be watching.

"We've got a few more months before that happens. Of course, I can think of plenty of other ways to warm up, if you're interested."

"You never give up, do you?" Honor would have laughed if she weren't so anxious to get in her car, get back to her house and hide inside again. She felt exposed, vulnerable and very aware of how easy it would be for someone to watch undetected.

It had been done before.

It was possible it was being done that very moment.

She shuddered at the thought, hurrying down the stairs next to Will. "I guess I'll see you tomorrow."

"See you then." Will continued through the parking lot while Honor half jogged to her own car. Fear made her pulse race and her hands tremble as she shoved the key into the lock. She really needed to get herself under control. Getting panicky wasn't going to keep her safe.

Headlights flashed as Honor opened her car door, and she looked up at the vehicle driving toward her. Not Will's car. He drove a Jeep. Someone else. Heading right toward her and flashing his high beams.

Honor yanked open her car door, her heart slamming against her ribs as she slid into the driver's seat. Her cell phone was in her pocket, and she pulled it out, her hand shaking so badly that she nearly dropped it on the floor. She needed to call the police. Though what good calling for help would do if the person in the car was carrying a gun, Honor didn't know.

The car pulled into the space beside hers, and Honor tensed, her fingers poised and ready to dial. As she watched, the interior light turned on, revealing sandy hair, strong features, eyes she knew were the same vivid blue as the flowers that bloomed in her mother's garden. Grayson.

She unrolled her window, relieved and frustrated at the same time. He'd scared five years off her life. "And just what are you doing out at this time of night, Grayson Sinclair? Besides scaring me to death, that is."

"Same thing as you. I just got finished working."

"Maybe so, but you weren't working here, so how did you end up in Lakeview Haven's parking lot?"

"It was on my way home from Lynchburg." The yellow interior light cast shadows beneath his eyes and added hollows under his cheeks. He looked hard and tough, and so appealing Honor almost had to look away.

"It was on your way home, so you thought you'd stop by? And you just happened to arrive as I was getting done?"

"The timing wasn't quite that perfect." He grinned, and Honor's heart jumped in response.

"No? Exactly how long have you been waiting?"

"One hour and fifteen minutes."

"Are you crazy?"

"That's up for debate."

"Really, Grayson, you should be home sleeping. Why wait out in a cold parking lot?"

"Why do you think? I wanted to make sure you got home in one piece."

"Grayson—"

"Look, I'm here. You're here. We're both heading home. Let's save the discussion of the reasons I shouldn't have done this for a time when we're not so tired." There was a weary edge to Grayson's voice that made Honor want to ask questions. Questions about his life, his work, his brother. Questions that shouldn't be asked by someone who wasn't interested.

And she wasn't interested.

No matter how much her heart might be saying otherwise.

"I guess I *am* tired. Let's go." She rolled her window up and pulled out of the parking lot, the headlights from Grayson's car reminding her of just how nice it was to not have to go it alone. Of just how comforting it was to have someone in her corner.

She closed her mind to the thought.

God was in her corner. She didn't need any more than that.

But maybe she wanted more.

Maybe she wanted to know what it would be like to let a man like Grayson into her life.

And maybe she was too tired and too scared to think straight.

Determined to change the direction of her thoughts, she turned on the radio, letting the soft classical music fill her mind and chase away the longings she didn't want to feel, but did.

THIRTEEN

Grayson's day hadn't gone well. Aside from the normal hectic pace of work and the hassle of trying to get several crews to work simultaneously on his parent's rental, he'd received a call from his father. Jude's condition had worsened, his weakened body attacked by a bacterial infection. According to his attending physician, the infection had been caught early and was under control, but Grayson still felt uneasy. He was worried about his brother, frustrated to be so far from him. He had wanted to take the next flight up to New York, but Jude had called before Grayson could buy the ticket and insisted that he didn't need another person hovering over his hospital bed.

Grayson knew his brother well enough to believe him. Jude had always been independent to a fault. Going his own way, forging his own path, determined to make decisions apart from the family. There was nothing wrong with that, but it had led him farther away from home than the rest of the Sinclair siblings. If Jude said he wanted Grayson to stay away, there was no doubt that he meant it.

Of course, there were other reasons Grayson hadn't flown to New York. Three of them. Honor, Lily and Candace

Malone. As long as Jude was holding his own and insisting he didn't need his brother at his bedside, Grayson would keep doing what he had been doing—keeping his eyes on the Malone women.

He rubbed the back of his neck, trying to ease the tension there as he followed Honor home. He hadn't meant to stop by Lakeview Haven, but he'd seen the sign for it on his way back from Lynchburg and had found himself traveling down the back road that led there. Compelled. Intent. Determined to help.

The night was silvery gray and silent, the moon pale gold as Grayson pulled into Honor's driveway and got out of his car. Honor's house was dark but for the light that illuminated the porch and cast shadows across the yard. Grayson surveyed the area as he approached her car, looking for signs that they weren't alone, that someone was watching from the darkness. There didn't seem to be anyone, but someone could be hiding out of sight, snapping pictures, getting ready to send another "gift" to the object of his affection.

The thought filled Grayson with rage, but he forced it down as Honor's car door opened. She had enough on her plate. The last thing she needed was to deal with his emotions.

He offered her a hand out of the car, and she hesitated before accepting, as if she were afraid letting him help would give Grayson an inroad into her life.

He didn't bother telling her that it was too late. That he was already too deep in to ever back out. She didn't need to deal with that, either. Eventually, there would be time for a discussion about their relationship, but that time wasn't now.

His hand tightened around hers as he pulled her from the car, and she smiled into his eyes. "Thanks."

"For what?"

"For following me home, though you really didn't have to."

"Sure, I did. Otherwise, I would have been lying in bed wondering if you'd made it into your house safely. Eventually, I would have given in and called to check on you. This saved us both some time."

"Well, now you know I'm home. Safe and sound. You can go back to your place and sleep peacefully. Good night, Grayson." Honor smiled at him, gently pulling her hand from his grip, her dismissal hinting that he was welcome to leave before she was inside.

"Not until I walk you to your door and make sure you're locked in tight."

"So, you really are a true gentleman?" There was laughter in Honor's eyes, and Grayson wondered what it would be like to know her under different circumstances. Wondered how she'd be acting, what she'd be saying if she hadn't been hurt before.

"I like to think so."

"Ah, but what *you* think in that regard doesn't matter. What matters is what others think."

"Then I guess I should be asking you."

"Whether or not you're a true gentleman? Right now it seems you might be." She smiled again as they moved up the porch stairs. "But it takes time to know the truth about someone."

"Then I guess we need to spend more time together so you can figure it out."

"I'm sure my opinion about you doesn't matter so much that I need to spend time figuring anything out. Or that you need to spend time worrying about what it is." She put her hand on the doorknob, and Grayson expected her to go inside.

Instead she turned to him, her eyes scanning his face, her brow furrowing. "I've been thinking about you today."

"Have you? Then maybe there's hope for us after all."

"Actually, my thoughts were centered more around your brother. How is he doing?"

Her question sobered Grayson, and he shook his head. "Not as good as I'd like. He's got a bacterial infection. The doctor is treating it aggressively, but Jude is pretty weak. It's hard to know what's going to happen."

"I'm sorry. I know how frustrating it can be when someone you love is sick." She touched his hand, her fingers lingering for a moment on his knuckles, their warmth searing into his skin, comforting him.

Grayson's pulse raced in acknowledgment. "What's more frustrating is that he doesn't want me up there with him."

"He's alone?"

"My parents are there. My sister and her husband are, too. And my brother and his wife. I've got another brother in Egypt who calls the hospital every day."

"No wonder he doesn't want you up there. He's being smothered by well-meaning loved ones." She leaned against the door, her dark hair falling over her shoulders, her eyes filled with compassion.

"I'm sure that's the way Jude sees it, but it's not the way we do."

"Of course not. You love him. You're not thinking how frustrating it is for your brother to have his independence taken away, or how demeaning it is for him to have his dignity lost to hospital gowns and catheters. And you're certainly not thinking about how hard it is for your brother to let all the people he loves see him weak and diminished."

"He's not diminished."

"Not in your eyes, but he is in his."

She was right, of course. Jude *would* feel diminished by his injuries. The hallmark of his personality was his independent spirit. "The fact that you're right doesn't make me feel better about being hundreds of miles away from him."

"I understand. I've spent a lot of time working with people who are going through similar things. Physical trauma doesn't only affect the person who's been hurt. The entire family suffers." She shivered and rubbed her arms. "It's cold and it's late. I'd better go in."

"Too bad. Talking to you is the best thing that has happened to me today."

She smiled and shook her head. "You really need to work on some better lines, Grayson."

"Who said it was a line?"

"I can't believe it's the truth. A man like you must have plenty of wonderful things happen every day."

"A man like me? What kind of man would that be?"

"Successful. Charming. Handsome."

"Somehow, coming from you, those don't seem like compliments."

"What else would they be?"

"Accusations."

"Why would they be that?"

"Because you've made it clear that charm and flattery go hand in hand and that neither are qualities worth admiring."

"What I admire or don't doesn't matter. You can't help what you are anymore than I can help what I am." She unlocked the front door. "Besides, I can think of much worse things to be than successful, charming and handsome."

"And much better ones?"

"I don't know about that. I suppose what someone finds admirable depends on what she's looking for." She stepped into the house, but Grayson put a hand on her arm before she could close the door.

"What is it *you're* looking for, Honor?"

"Nothing. Everything I need, I have. Now, I really do need to go. Lily gets up early, and I need to get some sleep before I begin another day."

"Good night, then."

"Good night to you, too, Grayson. And thanks again for escorting me home."

"Even though you really didn't need me to?"

"Maybe I did need you to, and I just didn't want to admit it." She started to close the door, but froze as the sound of a car engine filled the night.

Three houses up, headlights flared and a car pulled slowly into the street, easing toward Honor and Grayson with a deliberateness that made Grayson's muscles tighten. "Shut the door and call Jake."

"But—"

"Shut the door." He growled the words as he jogged down the porch stairs. The driver of the other vehicle paused in front of Honor's place, flaunting his presence with the kind of casual arrogance that was often the downfall of stalkers. Darkness hid the driver from view, but Grayson had every intention of putting a face and a name to the person behind the wheel.

He got in his car and started the engine, scowling and unrolling the window as Honor knocked on the passenger-side door. "Get inside the house."

"This isn't your battle to fight, Grayson. And I'd never forgive myself if something happened to you while you were chasing after that lunatic."

"Would you forgive yourself if Lily or Candace were hurt because of him?"

She blanched, but didn't step away from the car. "I won't let that happen."

"How will you stop it?"

"By coming with you to make sure you find him." She pulled the door open, slid into the seat.

Arguing would waste time they didn't have, so Grayson threw the sedan into Reverse and backed out onto the street.

The car they were following accelerated, taking a left turn and disappearing from view. If Grayson didn't hurry, he'd lose the guy. He stepped on the accelerator, adrenaline racing through his veins as he tried to close the gap between his car and the one he was following. For the first time since trading in the Jaguar, he missed it.

"Use my cell phone and call nine-one-one. Maybe the sheriff's department can cut this guy off before he gets to the highway. Tell them he's heading toward the Blue Ridge Parkway in a black sports car. No license plate."

Honor's fingers slipped as she tried to call the sheriff, her racing pulse and shaking muscles doing little to help the situation. She knew she sounded frantic as she relayed information to the 911 operator, but she didn't care. She should have listened to Grayson and gone back inside the house. Traveling at an excess of ninety miles an hour wasn't her idea of fun. Nor did she much like the idea of coming face-to-face with the man who was stalking her.

Up ahead, the car rounded a curve in the road, disappearing from view. Grayson followed, taking the curve a little too quickly. Honor expected to see taillights again, but the road was empty. "Where did he go?"

"He may have turned off his lights and gotten off the road. Or he might have pulled over to the side of the road to wait for us. We're outside of town in a rural area. In his mind, this might be a great place for a confrontation."

"Confrontation? I'm not sure I like that idea." As a matter of fact, she was confident she didn't.

"I do. I'm looking forward to having a little chat with the guy."

"Shouldn't you leave that to the police?"

"Only if they get to him before I do." Grayson's smile was hard and feral, and for the first time since she'd met him, Honor saw the iron will beneath the charm. The power. The ruthlessness. The determination.

He wouldn't give up on a goal. Wouldn't back away from a fight. He was the kind of man who could be a great friend or a bitter adversary. The kind of man Honor wouldn't ever want to cross. The kind she just might want to have on her side.

She shook her head, refusing to acknowledge the thought. Grayson was trouble. In more ways than one. As long as she kept that in mind, she'd be fine. "Maybe we should go home and let the police handle things."

"If we have a chance to stop this guy, we've got to take it. Men like him are unpredictable. First he sends anonymous gifts and now he's following you around. What will he be doing in a week? A month?"

"Sheriff Reed will find him before then." She hoped. She prayed.

"I've worked too many cases where that hasn't happened."

Grayson eased up on the accelerator, and the speedometer dropped from ninety to forty-five. "If our guy was waiting for us, we'd have seen him by now. He must have turned off. Let's backtrack. There's got to be a side road or driveway here somewhere."

"Grayson—"

"We're doing what we have to do to keep you and your family safe, Honor. There is no other option. You know that, don't you?" He met her eyes briefly before he turned his attention back to the road, and Honor saw the truth in his gaze. His need to protect, his concern. His integrity and honor. So many things she'd thought were impossibilities. There for the taking. If only she could believe they were real.

Her hands tightened into fists, her heart racing in her chest. Fear did funny things to people. It made them imagine things that weren't there. That's obviously what was making her see all the things she'd longed for written boldly in Grayson's eyes.

She continued to tell herself that as Grayson backtracked along the country road, found an old gravel driveway and turned onto it.

FOURTEEN

The gravel drive meandered through thick trees and ended abruptly at an overgrown clearing, a decrepit house standing forlorn and abandoned in its center. A sporty black car sat in front of it, shiny and out of place in the neglected clearing.

"Is that the car?" Honor whispered. Though why she felt the need to keep her voice down she didn't know. If the driver was still in the car, he'd seen them coming and knew they were there. Talking quietly wouldn't change that.

"Yeah. That's it, but it doesn't look like the driver is still in it."

"What do we do now?"

"We call for backup." He took the cell phone she was still clutching in her hand and dialed, speaking rapidly to the person who answered. Giving their location. Their situation. A description of the car.

And all the while, the clearing remained lifeless and black, the stalker's car a glaring reminder that a criminal lurked somewhere in the darkness.

By the time Grayson hung up the phone, Honor's nerves

were taut, her stomach tight with fear. She definitely should have done what he'd asked and gone back inside her house, locked herself inside and let other people deal with her troubles.

Should have.

Hadn't.

Now she was regretting it in a big way and praying that she'd get home to Lily and Candace in one piece.

"It's going to be okay. We're safe enough here." Grayson spoke quietly, his tone soothing.

"How can you say that? We're sitting in a car a hundred yards away from a lunatic's vehicle."

"He's not in it."

"That just makes it worse. He could be anywhere."

"He's as far away as his legs have been able to carry him."

"You don't know that." She crossed her arms over her chest, feeling vulnerable and scared in a way she hadn't since the days following Jay's death when she'd realized just how deep in debt he'd left her, and just how much her life was going to change.

"Sure I do. The guy is a coward. He skulks around in the dark shooting pictures of someone who doesn't know he's watching. Then he runs and hides. There's no way he's going to come out from wherever he's gone."

"He was brazen enough to drive by us while we were talking."

"Because he knew we couldn't see him. Men like him have agendas. They have plans. They don't veer from them. This guy has already chosen a time and day to meet you face-to-face. He's not going to want me around when that happens."

"That doesn't make me feel better."

"I didn't mean it to." Grayson shifted in his seat so that he was facing Honor, his eyes gleaming in the darkness, his face sharp angles and hard planes. "I've prosecuted men like this before, Honor. I know how they think. I know how they act. And I'll do anything I can to make you view the danger you're in as real."

"I do view it as real." More real by the minute.

"You don't. If you did, you'd have done exactly what I said and gone inside your house, locked the door and called the police."

"I couldn't let you come out here by yourself."

"You *should* have let me come out here by myself."

"I've told you before, Grayson. My problems aren't yours."

"And I've told you that I don't make promises I can't keep."

"Look—"

Grayson pressed a finger against her lips, sealing in her protest. "I hear sirens. Jake and his crew must be close."

"Do you always have to have the last word on a matter, Grayson Sinclair?" She huffed the words, her frustration with the man beside her spilling into her tone.

"Only when it serves a purpose."

"And exactly what purpose did it serve this time, I'd like to know?"

"You're not scared anymore, are you?" He got out of the car and closed the door before the words registered.

When they did, Honor wasn't sure if she should be angry or amused.

Or both.

She followed Grayson out of the car, relieved to see several police cruisers speeding into the clearing. Within seconds the once-dark yard was lit by spotlights, and uniformed officers were surrounding the stalker's car.

Not sure if she should get back in the car or stay put, Honor glanced around, searching for Grayson.

"Where's Gray?" Sheriff Reed strode toward her, his gaze probing the shadows at the far edge of the clearing before meeting Honor's.

"I don't know. He was here a second ago."

"Hopefully, he didn't go chasing after our perp alone."

"I don't think Grayson would do something like that." At least she hoped he wouldn't.

"He followed the guy here, didn't he?"

"Yes, but we waited in the car until we heard your sirens."

"*He* waited until he knew you'd be in good hands before he took off searching." The sheriff scowled, and Honor's stomach twisted with anxiety. Obviously, that was exactly what Grayson had done—waited until help arrived and then gone looking for the confrontation he'd talked about earlier.

"He's only been gone for a couple of minutes."

"Then maybe I can catch up to him. Get in the car and stay in the car until one of us comes back for you. Okay?"

She didn't think she had a choice, so Honor nodded and did as the sheriff asked.

Minutes ticked by as the activity in the clearing intensified. More police cars arrived. More people. More lights. The house lit up room by room, flashlights illuminating the dark interior. A van pulled up behind the car and a team of people began searching the sports car. From what Honor could see, they didn't find much.

A half hour passed. Then another.

Where were Grayson and Sheriff Reed? What was taking them so long? Had they found a trail to follow? Some sign that indicated which way the stalker had run? Or had something happened? A run-in they hadn't been expecting? An ambush? Were they hurt? Did they need help?

The questions circled around in her mind until she wanted to scream with frustration. She was too used to doing things on her own. She wanted to be outside the car, in the thick of things.

And she wanted to be home.

Safe.

Checking on Lily and Candace. Going on with her life the way it had been for so many years.

But she didn't think that would happen.

She didn't think things would ever be the same again. The tide had turned and she'd been turned with it. Struggle as she might, she'd never be able to free herself from its grip.

She shuddered at the thought, pulling her coat tighter and hugging her arms against her chest.

Where *were* they?

As if her question had conjured him, Grayson pulled open the driver's side door and got in the car, his expression dark and unreadable.

Relieved, Honor grabbed his arm, wanting to hold on tight so that he wouldn't leave again. "Thank goodness you're back. I was beginning to think something terrible had happened."

"Nothing terrible. Nothing good. Nothing, period." Grayson ground the words out, and then sighed, running a hand down his face. "Sorry. It's not your fault we came up empty."

"No apology needed. I'm just happy you're okay."

"Yeah?" He squeezed her hand and offered a smile that didn't reach his eyes. "I won't be happy until we find our guy."

"There was no sign of him?"

"I found some tracks and followed them to Summer Creek Road. It's a mile through the trees. After that, nothing. No tracks. No clue as to which direction he went."

"Could he have gotten a ride?"

"Anything is possible. Jake is going to call in a search team. They'll bring in their dogs, try to get a scent from the car and then see if they can catch his trail."

"And the car?"

"The state sent in their CSI unit. They've recovered a camera, but that's it. No papers. No old cups. Not even a fingerprint. The car is clean as a whistle and looks brand new."

"So we're at a dead end?"

"I'd say it's too soon to tell. I'd also say it's past time to get you home." He shoved the keys into the ignition and started the car.

"Should we tell the sheriff we're leaving?" Honor glanced out the window, searching for Sheriff Reed and finding him easily enough. He was standing near the crime scene van, talking to a tall, rail-thin woman.

"He already knows. He followed me to Summer Creek and read me the riot act for going it alone."

"And well he should have. You're a lawyer. Not a police officer."

"I'm a man before I'm a lawyer, and when a person I care about is in trouble, I don't wait around for someone to help me solve the problem." Grayson's sharp retort surprised Honor, and she put a hand on his arm, feeling the tension through his wool coat and wishing she could do something to ease it.

"I know. I didn't mean to imply otherwise."

"You didn't. I'm just frustrated that this guy slipped through my fingers. I can't believe I let him escape."

"You didn't let him do anything. I did. If I hadn't insisted on coming along, you would have gone after him sooner and found him."

"So, I can blame it on you, huh?" He glanced at Honor, and she saw the darkness in his eyes, the fury he was hiding beneath his smile. Despite his statement, she knew where his anger was directed—not at her for insisting she be included in the hunt, but at himself. He'd wanted to rescue Honor and her family, and he blamed himself for not being able to.

Something inside Honor shifted as she read the truth in his eyes. Some icy part that had grown around her heart in the years after she'd married Jay, when she'd realized that the one person she most wanted to trust couldn't be depended on.

She took a deep, steadying breath, refusing to believe what she knew was true—that Grayson was the kind of man she could trust. "I guess you can blame me, since I'm the one who slowed you down."

"I can't blame you for what you didn't intend." Grayson pulled up in front of Honor's house and turned off the car. "Besides, Jake was right. Rushing blind after someone who could have been carrying a weapon wasn't the smartest thing I've ever done."

"And insisting I come with you wasn't the smartest thing *I've* ever done."

"It seems neither of us are at our brightest tonight." Grayson's fingers brushed Honor's arm, coming to rest on her shoulder. His hand smelled of spicy cologne and cold winter nights, the scent masculine and compelling.

"Fatigue does funny things to people. Stealing their reasoning skills is just one of them." Honor knew she should get out of the car, go in the house and put the night behind her. Grayson's touch was light enough that she could move away, yet so comforting that she didn't want to.

"And can it make them imagine things?" He stared into her face, his expression unreadable, his eyes dark and somber.

"Like what?" She took a deep breath, trying to clear her thoughts and only succeeding in inhaling more of Grayson's scent. Her pulse throbbed in response, her skin heating.

"Like how soft your skin would be if I touched it?" His fingers skimmed down her cheek. "Because I've been imagining it all the way home. And you know, my imaginings didn't even come close to the reality of it. Your skin is soft as silk and warm as morning light."

"Grayson..." Her voice trailed off as his hand slipped beneath the hair at the nape of her neck, his fingers kneading the tender flesh there.

"Like you said, Honor, fatigue can do funny things to people. Maybe that's what's going on here. Or maybe something else is. And maybe that something needs to be explored." His lips barely grazed hers, and Honor's heart jumped, her pulse racing in acknowledgment. She'd forgotten the feel of a man's touch. The firmness of a man's lips pressed against hers. She'd forgotten how rational thoughts could fly away. How easily her defenses could be breached.

She backed away from Grayson, fumbling for the door handle. "I need to get inside. Good night, Grayson."

She hopped out of the car, racing up the porch stairs and into the house, running from things she didn't want to feel, from disappointments she didn't want to remember and from the man who seemed intent on dragging her back into the kind of relationship that could only lead to a broken heart.

FIFTEEN

The sun rose in fits and starts, first hidden by clouds, then revealed in golden beauty only to be hidden again. It reminded Honor of her life. The good and bad of it. The difficulties that were always followed by something wonderful. She stood on the back stoop, sipping a steaming cup of coffee and staring over the backyard, letting the cold autumn air swirl around her and watching as the sunlight peeked from the clouds and retreated again. Gold. Pink. Gray. Blue. There was no better place to be at dawn than outside. The silence, the peace, always made Honor feel closer to her Creator.

And right now, she desperately needed to feel that He was near.

She'd slept poorly again. Thoughts of the stalker had made it difficult to close her eyes. Thoughts of Grayson had made it difficult to keep them closed. She'd come to Lakeview with hopes of the kind of life she'd been dreaming of for years. What she'd gotten was something else entirely.

But maybe that was the point. Maybe her plan hadn't been God's. Maybe this was His way of showing her that. She could move back to St. Louis. There were plenty of nursing jobs there.

"But I don't want to, Lord. This place feels like home, and it's been a long time since anything has felt that way."

"Mommy?" Lily peered out from the open back door, her cheeks still flushed from sleep, her dark ringlets bouncing around her cheeks.

"What are you doing awake, my sweet?"

"Looking for you. I needed to tell you something."

"Something good?" Honor walked the few steps back to the house and shrugged out of her coat, letting it drop around her daughter's shoulders.

"No. Something scary." Lily's eyes filled with tears, and Honor pulled her into her arms.

"What is it, Lily Mae?" Fear made Honor's heart slam against her ribs and her arms tighten around her daughter.

"I saw the dragon last night."

Honor almost sagged with relief at the words. "Did you?"

"Yes. He was looking in the window while I was sleeping."

"If you were sleeping, how do you know he was looking in the window?"

"Maybe I wasn't sleeping. Maybe I was looking out the window."

"And why would you be doing that?"

"I wanted to see if Mr. Prince was home."

"You mean Mr. Sinclair."

Lily nodded, her blue gaze darting to Grayson's house.

"And this was after Candace put you in bed?"

"Yes."

"Lily, you know the rule. No getting out of bed after you've been put in it."

"I know, Mommy." She paused, placing her hand against Honor's cheek, her palm small and warm and too sweet for words. "But I was missing you, and I just wanted to see if Mr. Sinclair was home because that would make me less lonely."

"Candace was home with you. There was no need to be lonely."

"But Candace can't fight dragons." Lily said it as if it made perfect sense. To her it probably did.

"So you looked out the window and saw a dragon. Where was it? Near the swing set?"

"No. He was right there. Right near the window." Lily pointed toward the window, and a chill raced up Honor's spine. Had the stalker been outside her window again?

"What did he look like?"

"Black. And he breathed red fire."

"Fire?"

"Yes. Right at me."

"Oh my. That does sound scary." The more she heard, the less Honor believed that her daughter had actually seen something, but she set Lily down in the mudroom and retrieved her coat anyway. "Tell you what. You go get a juice box from the fridge while I go look for dragon prints."

"I want to come with you." Lily grabbed the hem of Honor's coat and seemed determined to hold on. Usually, Honor would have ignored her daughter's antics, but there was a frantic quality to them today that she couldn't disregard.

"All right. Put your coat and boots on and we'll go out together." She waited while Lily tugged on the fluffy pink coat she loved so much and shoved her sockless feet into snow boots. Her pink flannel nightgown fell to the floor, and Honor decided it would keep her warm enough for the few minutes it would take to check for footprints beneath the window. "Ready?"

"Yes."

"So, let's go exploring."

Clouds were covering the sun again as Honor led her daughter to the area beneath the window, the gray morning chill suddenly seeming more sinister than peaceful. Beneath the window, dry grass and weeds were matted down, but the entire yard was like that and Honor found nothing alarming at the sight. Frozen earth revealed no sign that someone had stood there, but Honor leaned close anyway, searching for some sign that what Lily had seen was more than imagination.

"Do you see any, Mommy? Do you see dragon prints?" Lily's whispered question was loud enough to send a squirrel racing up a tree, and despite her worry, Honor smiled.

"All I see is brown grass and weeds and dirt."

"That's because dragons fly. Maybe the dragon last night was flying. Maybe he didn't put his feet on the ground."

"Lily, I don't think you saw a dragon last night. At least not one that was breathing fire and flying."

"I did see him, Mommy. I really did."

Honor bit back a sigh of frustration. Whatever Lily had or hadn't seen, there had not been a dragon in the yard. "Maybe you saw something else."

"I saw a dragon. So tonight I want you to stay home. Okay? That way you can call Mr. Sinclair to come slay it if it comes back."

"You know I can't stay home tonight. People at work depend on me to be there."

"I depend on you, too, Mommy." Lily stared up into her eyes, her heart-shaped face and chubby cheeks making her look like a dark-haired cherub. Innocent. Sweet.

A child who needed her mother more than she needed anything else.

Honor rubbed the back of her neck, trying to ease the tension there. It was hard enough to leave her daughter every night. Having Lily beg her to stay just made it that much more difficult.

"Come here and sit on the swing with me." She lifted her daughter, ignoring the pain that speared through her lower back from too much time on her feet and too much tension.

She eased down onto one of the old swings, wincing a little as her muscles protested. Lily snuggled close, her head under Honor's chin, her arms wrapped around her neck. It wouldn't be long before Lily was too big to be held like this. A few years. A few inches. A few pounds. The little girl would be big. She wouldn't need Honor as much. And just like Candace, she'd begin to grow away. When that happened, Honor would be truly alone.

That was the way life was, and Honor knew it shouldn't hurt so much to think about. She pressed a kiss onto Lily's head, breathing in baby shampoo and innocence. "Did I ever tell you that when I was a little girl, I thought a troll lived under my bed?"

Lily shook her head, but seemed content not to speak. It was possible her fears had made her night as rocky as Honor's.

"Well, I really thought one did. Every night I'd climb into bed and hide my head under the covers because I was so afraid that the troll would come out. One day, I told Grandmom about the troll, and do you know what she said?"

"What?"

"She said there were no such things as trolls, but if there were, God's love was so big that when it was in a room, it chased everything else away. She said that since God loved me and was always with me, I never had to worry about trolls or anything else hiding in my room."

"But the dragon wasn't in my room. It was outside."

"There was no dragon outside, Lily. But sometimes there are scary things in the world. And you know what? God's love is so big that it can chase all those things away. Which does *not* mean that you should wander outside alone like you did the other day." She tickled Lily's belly, smiling as her daughter giggled.

When her giggles died away, Lily shifted in Honor's lap and stared into her eyes. "But God's love can't chase you away. Right, Mommy?"

"God's love only chases bad things away. When something is good, His love adds to it. And my love for you is very, very good. His love only makes mine stronger."

"And Candace's?"

"Of course."

"And Mr. Sinclair's?"

"Well, he doesn't know you very well yet, but if he did, I'm sure he'd love you, too."

"Of course I would. Lily is a very lovable little girl."

At the sound of Grayson's voice, Honor's heart skipped a beat. She whirled toward him, releasing her hold on Lily who was frantically trying to escape. Grayson stood a few feet away, near the shrubs that separated their property. Dressed in dark slacks, a white button-down shirt, a tie and a sports coat, he was immaculate, masculine and ready to face whatever the day brought.

Honor resisted the urge to smooth her flyaway hair or pull her coat tighter over her old cable-knit sweater and soft, faded jeans. "Grayson, I didn't hear you coming."

"Yeah. We'll have to talk about that another time." He met her eyes, and she knew what he was thinking—that she'd been foolish to come outside alone when a stalker was on the loose. She didn't agree. She'd been safe enough.

Until now.

Grayson's eyes narrowed as if he knew what she was thinking, and then he smiled. Full-out and charming, his teeth gleaming white, before turning his attention to Lily who was staring up at him as if Prince Charming had walked out of one of her fairy-tale books.

"Mr. Sinclair! Guess what?"

"What?"

"I saw a dragon last night. And he breathed fire and everything." Lily told her story in a voice loud enough to scare birds from the trees, but Grayson didn't seem to mind. He waited until she finished, then crouched in front of her and took both her hands in his. "I have a friend who might want to hear your story. Will you share it with him if your mom says it's okay?"

"Is he a prince?"

"No, but he loves stories."

"Okay." Lily bounced away, twirling in the gray morning light, her coat the only bright spot in the dreary yard.

"She's a cute little girl." Grayson lowered himself onto the swing next to Honor's.

"With a wild imagination."

"It may not have been her imagination."

"I know." Honor's throat tightened around the words, the fear she'd been trying to hold at bay rearing up and pulling her in.

"I want to bring Jake out here later. Let him listen to Lily's story. He's got a little girl. He might get kid-speak better than I do."

"All right."

"And I want you to stay in the house unless someone is

with you." He glanced at Lily who was hopping up and down the back stairs. "And I don't mean a four-year-old."

"You're not going to tell me I shouldn't have come out here this morning, are you?"

"What good would that do? You're already out here. Besides—" he leaned over and brushed hair from Honor's eyes, his gaze pulling her in, making her forget for a moment just how dangerous he was "—when I saw you and Lily out here it gave me an excuse."

"For what?" She asked even though she knew his answer was one she didn't want to hear.

"To see you again." The words hung in the air between them. Huge. Impossible to ignore.

But Honor *would* ignore them, because if she didn't, she'd have to admit that she'd been just as interested in seeing Grayson again. "And do you often go see neighbors at seven in the morning?"

"Only when they're already out in their yards. Though, I've got to say, it's a little cold out for visiting this morning."

Don't invite him in for coffee.

Do. Not. Invite. Him in.

Even as her mind shouted the words, Honor's mouth was opening and she found herself saying, "I've got a pot of coffee on. Would you like a cup?"

Grayson glanced at his watch and frowned. "I'd love to, but I've got a meeting at nine. I've got to grab some breakfast and get over to my parents' rental before then."

"I've got biscuits ready for the oven, and I'm making omelets. Why don't you join us for breakfast?"

What?

Had she lost her mind? Not only had she invited him for coffee, but now she was offering breakfast.

He wouldn't accept, of course. He'd already said he was busy. He'd head back to his house and Honor would go inside with Lily, and she'd never, ever do something so foolish again.

"Biscuits and an omelet sound great. I haven't had a home-cooked meal in weeks, but I don't want to impose."

"Pardon me?" Honor pulled her thoughts back to the conversation, not sure how the morning had gotten so completely out of her control. All she'd wanted was a few minutes of peace as the sun rose. What she was getting was trouble with a capital *T*.

"I said that I'd love to accept your offer, but I don't want to impose."

"If it was an imposition, I wouldn't have offered." She blurted out the words, knowing she sounded ungracious.

Grayson didn't seem to care. He stood, his light brown hair falling over his forehead, his eyes such a clear blue that it almost hurt to look in them. Clean-shaven, dressed for his meeting, he looked like exactly what he was—a successful, confident man. A man most women would be happy to invite for a meal.

Honor wasn't as enthusiastic, and it wasn't because she didn't see all the qualities in Grayson that other women would. It was because she *did* see them, and the more she saw, the deeper she fell. Soon, she'd be so deep that there'd be no climbing out.

"Then I guess I'll accept and not feel bad about it." He offered a hand, and Honor accepted, allowing him to tug her to her feet. She expected him to release his hold, but he just shifted his grip, linking fingers with hers as they walked to the back door.

She knew she should pull away, but somehow she found herself walking along with Grayson, enjoying the feeling of companionship his presence brought.

"Come on, Lily Mae. We're going to have some breakfast."

"With Mr. Sinclair?" Lily skipped up beside them, and grabbed Honor's other hand. Linked together, they walked up the back stairs and into the mudroom. To an outsider, they'd look like a family. Mother, father, child, heading back into the house after enjoying the sunrise together.

Of course, they weren't and just thinking in that direction made Honor uncomfortable.

She tugged away from Grayson's hold and stepped into the kitchen. "Go ahead and have a seat, Grayson. Everything will be on the table in ten minutes. Lily, go wash your hands and put on the clothes I laid out for you. But do it quietly. Candace is still asleep." She grabbed the apron her mother had always worn when she was cooking, the bright green one that had been handed to Honor the day she married Jay, and tied it around her waist, ignoring Grayson's raised eyebrows.

"What kind of omelet would you like?"

"What kind were you planning on making?"

"Vegetable. Peppers, onions and mushrooms." She pulled ingredients from the refrigerator and set them on the small counter.

"Sounds perfect to me. Can I help?" Instead of sitting at the table, he moved close, his chest brushing against her back as he leaned over to see what she was doing.

Honor's cheeks heated, her mind jumping back to the years when Jay had been alive. He'd always been content to read the paper while she cooked and had teased her good-naturedly when she wore her apron. It had been easy to have him in the kitchen, but Grayson was another story altogether.

He was a distraction, his scent and his warmth surrounding Honor as she diced onions. "You can put the biscuits in the oven for me. They're on the counter under that cloth. The oven is already preheated."

Any other day, Honor would have brushed melted butter over the biscuits before putting them in the oven, but today she didn't care about butter. She cared about putting some distance between herself and Grayson.

Grayson moved away, and Honor hurried to finish the onions. The sooner she finished, the sooner she could get Grayson fed and out of her kitchen. A kitchen that had seemed plenty big enough until he'd walked into it.

"All set. How long do you want me to set the timer for?" He spoke over his shoulder, and Honor had the feeling he wasn't nearly as affected by her as she was by him.

And why would he be? He probably dated all the time. Saw a different woman every week. Whereas Honor hadn't been on a date in years.

"Ten minutes is fine." She grabbed eggs, whisked them and poured them into a large skillet, working by rote, doing what she'd done hundreds of times over the years. It felt different, though. As if the gray world she'd been living in had bloomed into full color. Her senses were alive, her body humming with awareness.

Had it been like this with Jay?

She'd wondered that a lot lately, but she couldn't remember. The hard years, the years when Jay had spent money they didn't have on dreams that never panned out, the years when he'd made promises that he hadn't been able to keep—those years had wiped out the sweeter things. The gentle comfort that came from being together. The soft beauty of mornings spent sharing coffee and conversation.

Honor blinked back tears, refusing the sadness she knew she shouldn't feel. Jay had loved her. She had loved him. If they'd had time, they might have been able to forge something strong and unbreakable. They hadn't, and Honor couldn't spend her life regretting the things she'd never had with him.

"You look sad." Grayson moved up beside her, grabbing a knife from the cutting board and chopping a green pepper. He'd taken off his coat and rolled up his sleeves, revealing forearms that were tan and muscular. His hands were broad, his fingers long, and Honor vividly remembered the feel of them on her neck—warm and gentle.

She averted her gaze, concentrating on the mushrooms she was cleaning. "What do I have to be sad about? Any day my family is healthy and safe is a good one."

"Having a good day doesn't mean that we can't also feel sadness." Grayson dropped peppers onto the omelet, then stepped aside while Honor added mushrooms and onions. "So, what's on your mind that's making your eyes so dark and shadowed?"

"I don't think I'd like to be on the stand with you questioning me," Honor muttered as she folded the omelet and slid it onto a plate.

"Why's that?"

"You never give up. One question is always followed by another and another and another."

"How else can I find the truth?"

"It isn't always your job to do that." She poured more egg

into the pan, starting another omelet and refusing to meet Grayson's steady gaze. He read her too easily, saw more in her than she wanted to show.

"Just so we're clear—" he used his forefinger to tilt her chin, his eyes searching her face "—I don't think of you as a job."

Honor's heart stuttered as she remembered the warmth of his lips against hers. The brief, barely there contact that had left her longing for more.

It was definitely time to feed Grayson and send him on his way.

"Can you check on the biscuits? I think they may be done."

He looked as if he was going to refuse, but then he nodded, his finger dropping away from her chin as he turned and opened the oven.

She took a deep, steadying breath, trying her best to calm her pulse and her thoughts. What was wrong with her? Why was she so affected by Grayson? Had Candace's high school graduation and acceptance to college sparked an early midlife crisis?

Whatever the case, Honor needed to regain control and she needed to do it quickly.

The phone rang, the sound so surprising that Honor jumped and swung toward it. "Now who could that be at this time of the morning?"

"Want me to get it?" Grayson reached for the phone, but Honor shook her head.

"No. I will. Thanks." She lifted the receiver, half expecting to hear someone from work asking her to fill in for a shift. "Hello?"

"Tell your friend he'd better watch it. I don't like people

moving in on my territory. If he doesn't back off, he's going to wind up as dead as that lying, cheating husband of yours." The words were followed by a click, the line going silent as Honor's heart beat louder and harder in her ears.

"Is everything okay?" Grayson took the phone from her hand and placed it back on the receiver, studying her face as if he could read the answer to his question there.

Was everything okay?

No.

No, it wasn't okay.

A man, someone she didn't know, knew more about her than anyone should.

Your lying, cheating husband?

No one but Honor knew the truth of Jay's infidelity. She hadn't told her parents. Hadn't told her friends. Finding out at his funeral had only compounded Honor's grief, but she had felt no need to rehash the information. No desire to let other people know just how foolhardy her husband had been. And how naive she'd been.

Lying.

Cheating.

Jay.

She shook her head, trying to stop the words from echoing through her mind. But as soon as they stopped, others were there.

Tell your friend he'd better watch it.

He's going to wind up as dead as your lying, cheating husband.

Grayson. Her neighbor. Her friend.

More?

She reached for the phone, meeting Grayson's eyes, seeing

his strength, his determination, his integrity. All the things that had brought him into her life, and had kept him there. Had put him in danger. "No, everything isn't okay. I need to call the sheriff."

SIXTEEN

"You're absolutely sure that you never mentioned your husband's affair to anyone?" Jake Reed asked Honor the question for the fourth time in as many minutes, and Grayson ground his teeth to keep from telling his friend to stop beating a dead horse.

"I'd think I'd remember revealing something so personal." Honor's gaze jumped to Grayson, then dropped away again, her cheeks deep pink with embarrassment. Though what she had to be embarrassed about, he didn't know. Her husband had been a fool. Pure and simple. That was his sin, not Honor's.

Maybe she was embarrassed that Grayson had heard the truth? He was sure she would have been more comfortable if he'd left her alone while Jake questioned her.

He'd known it, but he'd stayed anyway.

There was something off about Honor's stalker. Something that didn't ring true. Grayson had been thinking about it most of the night...when he hadn't been thinking about Honor and the soft, sweet feel of her lips against his. The whisper of her breath as she'd allowed the contact between them.

He pulled his thoughts up short.

That was not something he should be dwelling on. Not now, at any rate.

What he *should* be concentrating on was putting the pieces of the puzzle together. Honor had lived in St. Louis for years. In all that time, she'd never had any indication that someone had taken undue interest in her. No flowers. No gifts. No notes left for her to find.

Nothing.

Then, in the course of a month, she'd been attacked in her apartment by a drug addict, moved to Lakeview and started receiving anonymous gifts and phone calls.

Had her picture been in the newspaper after the attack? If so, it was possible she'd been seen by someone who had created a fantasy relationship with her and had then followed her to Lakeview.

Stranger things had happened.

But the information the stalker had about Honor's husband put a crimp in that theory, and Grayson was growing more and more uneasy with the assumptions they were making about Honor's troubles.

Something was definitely off.

Honor had repeated the same information over and over again in answer to Jake's query—she'd told no one about her husband's affair.

Yet someone knew.

"What about your husband's military friends? Would they have been privy to the information?" Jake had a small notebook and was writing in it, but as he spoke he shot a questioning look in Grayson's direction.

More than likely, he was wondering why Grayson hadn't left. It was a good question, but one Grayson wouldn't answer.

Not unless Honor asked, and he knew she wouldn't. She preferred to pretend that their relationship was as simple as two neighbors getting to know each other.

"I'm sure they were. Jay was well liked. He had many friends. He wrote me several times after he went to Iraq, and he often included names of people he spent time with. It's possible some of them knew he was having an affair."

"Would it have been in character for your husband to share something so personal with people he knew?"

"If he thought they would keep the information from me, yes."

"Do you have the letters he wrote you?"

The color in Honor's cheeks deepened, and she shook her head. "I'm afraid I shredded them after the funeral."

"I can't say I blame you, but it would sure help if any of the names came to mind."

"I wish I could help you, but I can't remember much about the months before my husband died. I was quite pregnant and very caught up in getting ready for Lily's birth. After he died, I was just trying to put my life back together."

"You said Jay's girlfriend was at the funeral, and she made it very clear that she'd loved Jay and that he'd loved her." Grayson broke into the conversation, knowing neither Jake nor Honor would appreciate it, but not caring. He had questions, and he wanted answers. Asking was the only way to get them.

Honor glanced down the hall to the room where she'd sent Lily after the little girl had told Jake her dragon story. No doubt Honor was worried that her daughter would hear secrets that were better left hidden. "That's right."

"Who was there when she confronted you?"

"I don't know. It's been over four years."

"I know you'd rather not think about it, but any details you can give will help." Jake spoke with quiet authority, shooting Grayson more than a questioning look. This time he was clearly saying "back off."

Honor didn't seem to notice. She cocked her head to the side, her dark hair falling in a silky line over her shoulder as she stared into the past. "They'd already lowered the coffin into the ground. We'd thrown dirt on top of it. I was holding the flag I'd been given and staring down at my husband's coffin while everyone else began to wander back to their cars. That's when she approached me."

"No one else was around?"

"A few people were. Mostly military people. And Jay's mother and father, I think. They were there. I remember that very clearly because Candace had gotten in the car to avoid being near them, and I was relieved she hadn't been there to hear what was said."

"So maybe a half-dozen people heard?"

"Maybe."

"Do you have the name of the girlfriend?" Jake wrote something in his notepad, and Grayson knew he'd be contacting Honor's in-laws before the end of the day. The answer could lie in that direction. It was possible they remembered something Honor didn't. There was no way Jake would let that possibility go unexplored.

"I'm afraid not. She never introduced herself, and I didn't ask. Not her. Not any of Jay's friends. Once the funeral was over, I tried to put it all behind me. Jay was gone. There was no sense in holding on to anger over what he'd done."

"You're right about that, Ms. Malone. Although I've met

plenty of people who don't subscribe to the same idea." Jake closed his notepad and tucked it in his pocket.

"Forgiveness is something we're told to do. For others. For ourselves. For our relationship with God. I really didn't have a choice in the matter." Honor smiled, but the sadness Grayson had seen her eyes earlier was still there. Only now he understood it. And understanding made it all the harder to bear seeing.

He wanted to smooth the soft strands of her hair, wanted to tell her how much he admired what she was trying to do for her daughter and her sister-in-law. Wanted to say that protecting them by forgiving and moving on showed true courage and grace.

And he wanted to tell her that her husband had been pond scum.

But he didn't think she'd want to hear any of those things, so he remained silent as Jake asked a few more questions, issued a few warnings about staying safe and then headed for the front door. "I'm putting a patrol car at the end of your street until we find the guy who is stalking you. If something happens, we'll be close by."

The budget wasn't there for that, and Grayson wondered what Jake would offer his men to get them to volunteer for twenty-four-hour guard duty. Knowing Jake, it would be something good. Maybe a week's worth of vacation while Jake covered shifts. Grayson would ask his friend when Honor wasn't around, and then offer to help pay for whatever it was. Honor wouldn't be happy to know either of them had gone to the trouble, but in this case, what she didn't know wouldn't hurt her.

"I appreciate that, Sheriff."

"Jake. We've been seeing plenty of each other, so I'm

thinking it may be best if we're on a first-name basis. I'm going to check into some of the things you've told me. Contact your in-laws. Maybe see if I can get the name of your husband's girlfriend. Is that okay with you?"

"Sure, but I don't know what good it will do."

"I want to find the person who's stalking you. Any information anyone can give me about who might have known about your husband's affair will help with that."

"It's just been so long. I can't believe it's suddenly being dragged out and examined. If I'd known…" She paused, then shrugged. "But hindsight is always twenty-twenty, isn't it?"

"It is. And, for what it's worth, I think you made the right choice. Having a name wouldn't have changed what happened. I'm going to try to get a trace on your caller, but I'm thinking our perp made the call from a pay phone. Either that or he stole someone's phone and used it. No way would he be stupid enough to use his own."

"If he did, it would make your job easier." And make Grayson a whole lot happier.

"So far he hasn't done much to give himself away. But eventually he'll slip up. That's when we'll get him."

"What about the car he was in last night?" Honor's face was pale and tightly drawn, and Grayson briefly wondered how many more days of this she could take.

The answer was obvious—as many as it took. That was Honor's personality. It was her gift. To work toward a goal with determination and drive, but with her gaze always focused on others, her purpose always to serve rather than be served.

"Nothing from CSI yet, but we're trying to trace the car to its dealer. If we're able to, we may find out who purchased it." Jake stepped outside, letting bitterly cold air into the house. In the distance, dark clouds pressed low against the Blue Ridge Mountains. "On a lighter note, my wife and I are having a birthday party for my daughter next month. She's turning four. My wife would love for you to bring Lily."

"That's very sweet of her. I know Lily would love to come."

"You can bring your sister-in-law, too. We've got a dozen college students in our young-adult class at church. It might be nice for Candace to meet them. I'll tell Tiffany to go ahead and send the invitation." Jake paused with his hand on the cruiser's door. "Grayson, I think we need to talk later."

"Do you?" Grayson leaned against the doorjamb, not nearly as anxious to have a discussion with Jake as his friend seemed to be to have one with him.

"Yeah. Your life has been threatened. I don't take that lightly."

"Neither do I, but I think Honor is in a lot more danger than I am."

"How about we meet for lunch anyway? We'll discuss measures I want you to take to stay safe."

"Sure, but if those measures include staying away from Honor, forget it."

"I'm due for some time off. I'll drive out to your office. We can go from there."

"See you then." Grayson waited until Jake pulled away before turning to Honor. She was watching him, her eyes filled with fear.

"He's right, you know. You *are* in danger. Because of me. I think it would be best if—"

"I'm not going to stay away, Honor. Nothing you or Jake or your stalker say will convince me to do that."

"If something happens to you because of me…" She shook her head. "I couldn't live with that, Grayson."

"You won't have to. Your stalker isn't the first criminal I've angered. He won't be the last."

"Just be careful, okay?" She grabbed his hand, her touch sending heat through him.

"You don't need to worry about that, Honor." He brushed hair from her cheek, his palm resting against silky flesh. "I'll be as careful as you are going to be."

"Then I guess I'll be very, very careful." She stepped away from his touch, putting distance between them that Grayson didn't want. "Do you think any of the information I've given the sheriff will help him find the stalker?"

"If anyone can find answers, it's Jake. He's like a dog with a bone. He'll never give up. Not until he gets what he wants."

"I hope you're right. That phone call this morning…" She shook her head.

"What?"

"It was like a stranger had stepped into my life and stolen something sacred to me. The secrets closest to my heart." She frowned, her gaze on the distant mountains and the darkening clouds.

"You've been through a lot in the past few years, Honor. You deserve to keep whatever secrets you choose."

"Maybe. Maybe not. But I'd at least like to have a choice about whom I share them with." She rubbed her arms and Grayson pulled her close, wrapping her in his coat.

For a moment, her hands rested on his shoulders, and he was sure she planned to push him away. Instead, her palms settled tentatively, her touch so light it was barely there.

Like the kiss they'd shared.

Like the longing that seemed to have settled into Grayson's soul. A quiet whisper that said that this was the right place, the right woman, the right time and he'd be a fool to walk away.

Honor sighed, settling more deeply into his arms, her hair soft as silk against his chin, her warmth seeping through his shirt, heating his skin, the scent of summer drifting around them.

"Honor?" Candace's spoke quietly, but Honor jumped as if she'd shouted, pushing against Grayson's arms and turning to the open front door, her cheeks cherry red.

"Yes?"

"I hate to interrupt, but I've really got to get going or I'll be late for class." Candace's words were directed to Honor, but it was Grayson she was eyeing with curiosity he didn't miss.

"And I've still got to feed Lily. Breakfast got interrupted by the sheriff's arrival. Have a good day, Candace. It looks like a storm is coming in, so drive carefully." The words spilled out in a breathless rush, and then Honor was running into the house, carrying the scent of summer with her.

"Well, that was awkward." Candace smiled at Grayson, a hint of amusement in her eyes as she looked him up and down, searching, Grayson thought, for flaws.

"Why?"

"Because it's Honor. She doesn't 'do' men." Candace hitched a backpack onto her shoulder and started down the porch steps.

"She married your brother."

"Yeah. Poor thing. Not only did she get stuck with a lying, cheating rat, but she ended up with me." Candace smiled again, but there was no mistaking the truth in her words.

"She loves you."

"She loved my brother, too. That didn't make living with him easy. He was like my dad. All polished and pretty on the outside, but stuffed with rotting, fetid things. Both were parasites who lived off the people around them. My mom had money my dad fed off. Jay fed off Honor's love. Taking and taking and never giving back. If he hadn't died, Honor would have found out the truth and it would have ruined her. At least this way, she's been able to make a life for herself." She shrugged too-slender shoulders, the gesture so much like Honor that Grayson could almost believe the two were related by more than name.

"She would have tried to make it work. You might have all ended up a happy family."

"Please, Mr. Sinclair, you don't know my family. We're cursed. The men are always brutes and the women are always doormats. No one is ever normal. And no one even knows the meaning of the word 'happy.'"

"I'm sorry things were so tough for you, Candace."

"It's water under the bridge now. I just pray every day that I won't end up like my biological family."

"You won't."

"No? I'm sure my brother thought the same thing before he cheated on the only woman who ever loved him." Candace climbed into an old Chevy and drove away before Grayson could ask her for more information.

What he'd gotten wasn't nearly enough.

Candace knew that Jay had cheated on Honor.

Had she just found out, or was it something she'd known about for years?

And if it was, had she told anyone else?

The answer would have to wait until later. Grayson had a meeting in—he glanced at his watch—forty minutes. If he didn't hurry, he'd be late.

And if he stayed on Honor's front porch any longer, he might just decide he didn't care.

He chose not to knock on the door and walk back through Honor's house. Instead, he walked around to the back and crossed the tangled mess that passed for a yard. He had a lot on his plate today. Plenty that needed to be dealt with. Not the least of which were his brother's accommodations. The bacterial infection was clearing; Jude was getting better. According to Grayson's parents, that only made their police veteran son more difficult to deal with. A week, two at the most, and then Jude would arrive in Lynchburg. Making sure everything was ready was Grayson's priority.

Or one of them.

Honor had become a priority, too.

And just like the previous night, Grayson planned to be waiting for her when she got off work, planned on making sure she got home safely. Honor might not "do" men, but she needed Grayson. Whether she wanted to admit it or not.

And Grayson was beginning to believe he needed her, too.

A woman like Honor could ground him. In faith. In family. In all the things he'd always known were important, but that had somehow gotten lost in his rush to get ahead.

God's plan?

Grayson was starting to think so, and he was beginning to believe that the path he'd taken, the one he'd thought had brought him too far away from God to ever lead him back, had come full circle. That the things he'd once valued, the things he'd been so sure he'd never have, were within his grasp. All he had to do was have the faith to go after them.

SEVENTEEN

Rain poured from the sky as Honor hurried to her car. The night shift had been brutal, with one of Honor's Alzheimer's patients going into cardiac arrest. Despite every effort, the seventy-year-old had passed away en route to the hospital. Death was as much a part of her job as life, but Honor never got used to it, and the cold rain and deep black night only reminded her of how sad the night had been.

She waved goodbye to William and slid into her car, anxious to get home. Lily hadn't wanted her to leave, and there had been tears. That was unusual enough to worry Honor. Her daughter wasn't one to cry and whine. Like her father, she was quite good at taking life in stride.

Jay.

He'd been on her mind way too much lately. She knew why. Being with Grayson reminded her of what she'd thought she would have when she'd married her husband—a shoulder to lean on; someone to depend on.

It also reminded her of betrayals she'd rather forget.

Sharing the story of Jay's infidelity had been painful. Sharing it in front of Grayson had made her want to climb into bed, curl up under her covers and hide her head in shame. The rational part of her told Honor that Jay's sin had been his own. The other part whispered that if she'd been a better wife he never would have strayed.

Foolishness, she knew, but painful anyway.

She pulled out of the parking lot and started toward home, tensing when a car pulled out behind her. Headlights flashed. Once. Then again. Some kind of signal that she couldn't even begin to understand. Whoever was following her had been waiting in the parking lot, biding his time until Honor was alone.

Her pulse raced and she pressed on the accelerator as she fumbled in her purse and pulled out her cell phone. It rang before she could flip it open, and Honor screamed, nearly dropping it in her surprise.

Could the stalker have gotten her cell phone number? Was it possible he was behind her, calling to taunt her before making his move? "Hello?"

"Ms. Malone?" The female voice surprised Honor, and her fear was replaced by anxiety. Phone calls didn't come at three in the morning. Not good ones, anyway.

"Yes?"

"This is Deputy Raintree. I'm with the Lakeview sheriff's department."

"Is everything okay? Are the girls okay?" Honor's heart beat a terrible rhythm, hard and harsh and uneven. There were things she never let herself think about. Things that were too horrible to even contemplate. Losing the girls was one of them.

"I'm sure they're fine, Ms. Malone. I'm calling about the car that is following you."

"What?" Honor glanced in the rearview mirror and eased up on the accelerator.

"The car that's behind you. Mr. Grayson Sinclair is driving.

He asked me to call and let you know that he's providing an escort home."

"He could have called me himself."

"He didn't have your cell phone number. We had it on file here." Was this woman for real? Or was this an elaborate scheme to get her to let down her guard? Honor glanced at the caller ID on the cell phone, saw the sheriff's department listed as the caller.

Okay.

Maybe she had let her imagination get the best of her. Obviously, the police weren't in on the stalker's scheme.

"Are you sure it was Grayson you spoke with?" Honor glanced in the rearview mirror again. "Anyone could have called and asked you to contact me."

"Ma'am, I've known Grayson Sinclair for six years. It was definitely him. As a matter of fact, he promised me a box of Godiva chocolate if I did this favor for him. You tell him, I'm holding him to that."

"Right. I'll do that."

"And give him your cell phone number, will you? Sheriff Reed doesn't pay me to make personal phone calls." The deputy was laughing as she hung up the phone.

Honor wasn't quite as amused.

Grayson had taken years off her life. Worse, in the short time she'd known him, he'd already become an expected part of her day. Sure, she'd been surprised to hear he was the one in the car behind her, but a small part of her had almost expected it. Like being told the golden light on the horizon was the sun, the deputy's news had made perfect sense.

She drove home slowly, mindful of the slick road and the pouring rain, and just as mindful of Grayson following behind. Not too close. Not too far away. The fact that he'd come to Lakeview Haven again, had waited until her shift was over and followed her home, these were the kind of things she'd once longed for from Jay. Her husband had seen her as a strong, capable woman. That had been both a blessing and a curse. While he'd trusted her to handle whatever problems came their way, he'd also counted on her to do so. The responsibility for the well-being of their family had always rested squarely on her shoulders. She'd told herself that it was okay, had tried to convince herself that Jay's willingness to let her handle things was a compliment. Often, though, it had felt more like a burden.

More thoughts about Jay.

More memories she'd wanted to keep buried.

She'd thought she'd forgiven him and let go of the anger that had filled her when she'd learned of his betrayal, the anger that had eaten at her soul when she'd realized the debt he'd left her. Realized she'd have to move out of her house and rent an apartment in order to pay the bills he'd accrued.

Maybe she hadn't, because when she thought of him now, she could only think of the bad memories. Never of the good times. But, then, there had been so few of those.

She passed a marked police car parked at the end of her street and pulled into her driveway, exhausted and frustrated by her thoughts. In the past month, her life had gotten completely off track and she wasn't sure how to get it back on again. She wasn't even sure she knew what the "right" track was. Moving, getting a new job, providing for her girls. Those things were givens. They were already done and nothing could change them.

But what now?

That was the question she couldn't answer until the predator who was hunting her was found. Things were too confusing. Too unbalanced.

She opened the car door, icy pellets of rain sliding down her hair and into her coat collar. Winter gloom had ruled the day and had given the night an arctic chill. Honor hurried onto the porch, waiting beneath its sheltering roof as Grayson got out of his car and followed. His hair was mussed, his shirt open at the collar, his tie hanging loose around his neck. He looked tired.

And much more handsome than any man had a right to be.

Every woman in the courtroom must dream of romance and love when Grayson walked in. Honor could picture the female jurors so caught up in watching the handsome prosecutor, they forgot to pay attention to the evidence.

She smiled at the thought.

"What?" He brushed rain from his hair and rubbed his hand down his jaw, the gesture speaking of a weariness that Honor understood only too well.

"I was thinking that you must be a distraction in the courtroom, what with that *GQ* model thing you've got going on."

"Were you?" He smiled, his eyes flashing with surprise and something else. Something deeper and more compelling.

"Yes. I think someone should make it illegal for the prosecutor to overshadow the evidence."

Grayson's laughter was deep and warm, washing over Honor and reminding her that life didn't always have to be a serious thing. That sometimes laughter could make the most difficult times bearable. "I'll have to tell Jude you said that. He'll laugh himself to good health in no time."

"They do say laughter is the best medicine."

"My point exactly."

"How is your brother doing? Have you gotten an update?"

"Marginally better. Lord willing, he'll be headed this way in a couple of weeks." Grayson yawned, smiling apologetically. "Sorry. Long day."

"Don't I know it?" Honor unlocked the door, but stopped short of opening it. "I would think you'd have gone straight home to bed rather than waiting to escort me here."

"I wouldn't have slept anyway. Not until I knew you were home safe. I'm sure I mentioned that before." He took a step closer, and Honor could almost feel his warmth through her coat. She tried to back up, and bumped into the door.

"You can't escort me home every night, Grayson. You know that, don't you?"

"What I know is that you're a woman in danger, and having me around might just keep you safe. That being the case, everything else is moot."

"I keep trying to tell you that I'm not your responsibility."

"And I keep trying to tell *you* that I always keep my promises."

"Are we going to have this conversation every time we see each other?"

"That depends."

"On?"

"Whether or not you stop telling me I shouldn't do what I know is right." He smiled, but there was grim determination in his eyes, and Honor knew he meant what he said. Somehow, he'd convinced himself her well-being was his responsibility. Nothing Honor said would change his mind.

She decided to try anyway, because Grayson's presence was too unsettling, too alarming.

Too addictive.

And it was the kind of addiction Honor wasn't sure she'd want to break. "I appreciate your concern, Grayson, but there's a police car parked a few hundred yards away. I don't think either of us need to be worried about my safety."

"There aren't officers lined up on your route home, Honor. And a lot can happen on a ten-mile stretch of road." He sounded as tired as Honor felt.

"A lot can happen if I do something stupid. Like stop to help a stranded motorist or pick up a hitchhiker. I can assure you I've got no intention of doing either of those things."

"I'm sure you don't."

"Then stop staying up until all hours of the night to protect me. Not getting enough sleep isn't healthy."

He chuckled and shook his head. "Not healthy? If you knew what I ate today, you wouldn't be so worried about how much sleep I'm getting."

"Should I ask what you've been eating?"

"Today? Since our breakfast was interrupted, I got a doughnut on the way to my meeting, then I grabbed a hamburger and fries while Jake lectured me on keeping out of his investigation."

"He lectured you?"

"I'm afraid so."

"And you listened?"

"He was buying lunch, and I was hungry." Grayson sounded disgruntled, and Honor laughed.

"Poor you. What else did you eat today? Besides fast food junk."

"A taco."

"Fast food?"

"Is there any other kind when you've got a busy schedule?"

"Yes. And you're right, your eating habits are as unhealthy as your lack of adequate sleep."

"Actually, I did sleep. For about two hours while I was waiting for your shift to end. The sound of your car engine woke me up."

"Be that as it may, you still need to get home and into bed. Your busy day will start all over again very soon."

"What I need—" he smiled and took a step closer "—is a good home-cooked meal or two. That'll get me back on track with the right nutrients."

"It'll be good for you to cook one, then."

"And here I was hoping to get another invitation." Grayson's laughter shivered along Honor's spine, making her want to lean in and rest her head on his chest, feel the vibration of it against her cheek.

"Sorry, but I always try to learn from my mistakes."

"Is that what this morning's invitation to breakfast was?"

"And yesterday."

"You mean the kiss that wasn't?"

"It most certainly *was*."

"No, Honor. It wasn't. This—" he took a step closer, closing what little space had been between them "—is a kiss."

And then he showed her, his lips pressing against hers, firm and tender all at the same time. His scent surrounding her, his hands settling on her waist.

And for a moment, she lost herself to his touch. Allowed herself to forget all the reasons why letting Grayson kiss her was a mistake.

Breathless, she pulled away, staring up into Grayson's eyes and seeing her own confusion and worry reflected there. "We need to stop this now before one of us gets hurt."

"There's no reason why that should happen."

"Of course there is. Isn't that always the end result of these kinds of things?"

"What kind of thing are we talking about?"

"Men and women getting to know each other. Dating. Falling…for each other."

"It's not always the end result. Sometimes people build something great and lasting. Sometimes they make a lifetime together."

"Sometimes." But not this time, because Honor couldn't risk her heart for something that might not ever be.

"You don't think it will be like that for you?"

"I tried for a lifetime before, Grayson. With a man I'd known and admired and fallen in love with. We were best friends before we married and best friends after, but even that wasn't enough to make it work."

"It takes two committed people to make something work."

She knew what he wasn't saying—that it was obvious Jay hadn't been committed. She didn't comment on it though, because it was late and she was tired. Because saying it wouldn't change anything. Because it was time to say goodnight to Grayson. And goodbye. "Thank you for the escort, Grayson, but I'd rather you not bother tomorrow. I've been doing things on my own for a long time and, really, that's how I prefer it."

He stared at her for moment, his eyes dark as a storm-filled cloud. Then he nodded. "All right, Honor. But just so you know, sharing a road isn't the same as offering an escort."

"I—"

"You were right when you said I needed some sleep. Go on inside or I'll never get home."

Honor thought about saying a hundred different things, but in the end she said nothing but good-night. There was nothing she could say that would change what was happening. Nothing she could do to convince Grayson that there was no attraction between them. Nothing she could do to convince herself that she didn't want to see him again.

She closed the door and turned the lock, waiting until Grayson's car engine purred to life, the sound slowly fading, before she turned and walked down the hall.

EIGHTEEN

Honor expected both girls to be asleep when she walked into the house, and she crept down the hall silently, hoping to keep it that way. Lily hadn't been sleeping well lately, and the last thing Honor needed was to have to deal with her daughter's imagination. It could take an hour to settle Lily in again if she decided she needed to be up and talking about her prince or her dragon or any other fantastical thing that her four-year-old mind could conjure.

Determined to get into bed as quickly as possible, Honor almost ignored the bright light that was spilling out from under Candace's door. Her sister-in-law might be up studying, or might have fallen asleep with the lights on. In either case, she was eighteen and didn't need to be checked on. Old habits were hard to break, though, and Honor knocked gently, not really expecting an answer, but knowing she wouldn't be content to go to sleep without making sure Candace was okay.

"Come in." Her sister-in-law's voice sounded muffled, and Honor pushed open the door, concerned when she saw Candace curled up on the bed, still dressed and facing the wall.

"Is everything okay, Candace?"

"The sheriff left a message on the answering machine. He didn't want to call you at work."

"About what?" Honor crossed the room and sat on the edge of the bed. She knew her sister-in-law well enough to know that she couldn't rush the truth out of her. Whatever was wrong, Candace would let her know in her own good time.

"Mom."

"Mom?" It had been a long time since Honor had heard Candace mention the woman who'd raised her until she was thirteen.

"Yeah. You know. The woman who was happy to get rid of me. The one who said I was too much trouble to have at home."

"What about her?" Honor brushed thick bangs out of Candace's eyes, trying to read her expression.

"She's dead."

"Oh, honey, I'm so sorry."

"I'm not." A single tear slid down Candace's cheek and soaked into her bedspread.

"I know you don't mean that."

"I do mean it."

Honor knew better than to argue. Candace's emotions could rage as wildly as a forest fire, but they always died down quickly. She'd broach the subject again, once Candace had time to deal with what she was feeling. "Did the sheriff say what happened?"

"He just left a message saying you should call him. Of course, I know what happened. She drank herself to death. She always cared more about her vodka than anything else." Candace's words held a lifetime of bitterness and pain.

"She cared about you, Candace. I know she did."

"How could you possibly know that? She never did one

thing to show it." Another tear fell, and Honor's heart broke for her sister-in-law.

"Did the sheriff speak to your father? Did he leave a number where we could reach him?" Chad Malone hadn't spoken a word to Honor at his son's funeral. Nor had he acknowledged his daughter. His wife, Melanie, had been silent, too, her blue eyes faded and blank as if life had taken everything she had to give.

"No. All the sheriff said was that Mom has been dead for two weeks. Even if he'd left a number, I wouldn't want to call my father. Two weeks. And he couldn't even let me know."

"Candace…" Honor's voice trailed off as she tried to think of the right words to say. The fact was, it had been Candace's choice to break ties with her family. There had been phone calls from Melanie during the first year after Candace had moved in with Honor and Jay, but Candace had always refused to speak to her mother. Paid airline tickets had gone unused because Jay hadn't seen a reason to force his sister to visit her parents, who had made it clear she wasn't wanted. Honor had tried to change both her husband's and her sister-in-law's minds with no success.

After a year, the phone calls had stopped. There had been no more talk of visits. Candace had been relinquished completely, but Honor had known that her sister-in-law had never truly let go of her parents or the past she'd shared with them.

"She wasn't a good mother, Honor. Not like you. She drank to forget and she forgot a lot. But she was still my mother." Candace's words were barely audible, and Honor smoothed a hand over her hair, wishing she had words that would take away the pain her sister-in-law was feeling.

"And she loved you in her own way, Candace."

"You're sweet, but she didn't. Not as much as she loved other things. One of the most important lessons I've learned from you is that true love has no limitations or boundaries. It goes on despite time or distance. No matter what. My mother's love was never like that. If it had been, she never would have let me go."

Tears burned behind Honor's eyes, and she patted Candace's shoulder. "And one of the things I've learned from you is that the unexpected things in life are often the most wonderful. Another thing I've learned is that the best kind of sister is a sister of the heart, and that's what you are to me, Candace. Truly."

"Thanks." Candace's smile was a quick curve of her lips, gone before it was ever really there.

"I'll call the sheriff first thing in the morning and find out what happened."

"I don't need to know. I don't want to know." But she did, and Honor could feel it.

"Maybe he can give me your father's address and phone number. We could call—"

"No!" Candace bit her lip, and then continued more quietly. "My mom was a lost soul. My father was evil. I don't want anything from him. Not even answers about what happened to my mother."

"Candace—"

"I'm really sorry, but I'm tired and I've got school tomorrow. So, if you don't mind, I'd rather not talk about this anymore."

Honor wanted to continue the discussion, but knew it would lead nowhere. She'd learned long ago that conversations about Candace's childhood were off limits. It had been the same with Jay. He'd told her just enough to help her understand why he wouldn't say more.

"All right. If you want to talk, I'm always ready to listen."

"I know. Good night, Honor."

"Good night." Honor reached for the light switch, but Candace levered herself up in bed.

"Leave it on, okay?"

"Sure." Honor closed the door, tears clogging her throat and filling her eyes. It hurt to see Candace in pain and to know that there was nothing she could do about it.

Antsy, anxious and wishing it were a decent hour so she could call Jake, get her father-in-law's number, do *something,* Honor went to the kitchen, made a cup of tea and sat at the table. Rain tapped against the windows and roof, the sound a soothing reminder of spring in Ireland and the subtle scent of grass and flowers drifting in the open windows of her parents' home.

She missed those days, but more than that, she missed the sense of security she'd always had there. Since Jay's death, Honor's life had been about paying bills, paying off debts and keeping the household afloat. Enjoying the simple pleasures of spring rain or winter snow had become more difficult than Honor had ever imagined. Balance. Prioritizing. Those were things Honor was always struggling with. It wouldn't be so bad to have someone share that burden with her. It wouldn't be so bad to believe that Grayson was right and that a lifetime could be made by two committed people. Her parents had done it. Some of her friends had been married for a decade or more.

And Honor had been married for six years to a man who'd never seemed committed to anything more than himself. She'd been so naive, so sure that love could conquer all. It couldn't. It could only open a person up to pain, to heartache and to disappointment.

She rubbed the ache in her lower back and sipped

chamomile tea, wishing the past didn't seem so much a part of the present lately. Hearing that Melanie had passed away only added to the worry she'd been feeling. The news would have to be dealt with. She'd have to contact Candace's father to offer condolences no matter how Candace felt about it.

Not that he necessarily needed condolences.

From everything Jay had told her, Melanie and Chad Malone had had a rocky relationship filled with knock-down, drag-out fights. Still, after so many years of marriage, Chad must feel some grief over his wife's death.

Maybe.

But Honor knew enough about her father-in-law to recognize that Candace's words were a little too close to the truth. Chad wasn't evil, but he was empty. The kind of person who needed more and more to fill the hollowness inside. A black hole of emotion that sucked everything in and never let go.

Honor hadn't needed to spend a lot of time with the man to realize that. All she'd had to do was watch how he treated his wife and his children.

She sighed and stood to pace across the room and stare out the window. In the distance, a single light burned through the rain and the darkness. She knew whose it was, and the temptation to pick up the phone and call him filled her.

Such a dangerous longing, the need to share her thoughts and concerns with someone else.

Her fingers tightened on the teacup, and she turned away.

"I don't need Grayson Sinclair, Lord. What I need are answers. I need to find out who's been stalking me. I need to find out what happened to Melanie so I can give Candace some sense of closure. I need to get settled in and I need to move on, but I don't need Grayson." She whispered the prayer out loud, sure that God heard, but not sure He agreed.

Since the day she'd become a Christian when she was eight years old, Honor had understood that God had a plan and a purpose for her. She'd believed that the people that came into her life, the circumstances she faced were all part of His plan. Time and experience hadn't changed her mind or altered her faith, but they had forced her to accept that sometimes she wouldn't know all the reasons behind the things that happened to her.

It was possible, even probable, that God had put Grayson into Honor's life for a reason. Whether that was to keep her safe, or for some other reason, she didn't know. What she knew was that she wasn't comfortable with it.

She'd made up her mind about men a long time ago.

She didn't plan to change it.

But maybe God did.

The thought didn't comfort Honor as she put the teacup into the sink and retreated to her bedroom. She had a lot to do tomorrow. Calls to make. Errands to run. A man to avoid.

Somehow she thought the last would be much more difficult than the others.

NINETEEN

By ten the following morning, Honor had called Jake and gotten Chad's address and phone number. Florida. Honor had never imagined her Houston-born in-laws would move from their home state. Though, in the time after Jay's death they had moved from the suburbs of Houston to a country estate. Honor had lost track of them after that, her Christmas cards had been returned two years in a row. She'd had too much going on to worry much about where her in-laws were or what they were doing. They had known where she lived. She'd made sure to inform them as soon as she moved to the apartment in St. Louis.

The fact that they hadn't been courteous enough to do the same when they'd moved hadn't surprised her, and Honor had spent little time thinking about it.

Obviously they hadn't wanted to.

She glanced at the paper she'd left on the kitchen table, Chad's phone number written in black marker. All she had to do was pick up the phone and dial, but the thought of doing so filled her with dread. She'd spoken to Chad only three or four times, but it was enough for her to know that she'd rather not speak with him again. For Candace's sake, she'd do it.

But not yet.

She pulled stew beef from the refrigerator, poured oil into a pan and coated the beef with flour. Outside, rain continued to fall, soaking the yard so that brown, weed-filled puddles formed. Soft music drifted out of the dining room where Lily sat coloring pictures and listening to her favorite Kids' Praise CD. Why ruin such a peaceful morning by calling a man who knew nothing about peace?

Because it had to be done, that's why.

When Candace came home from classes, Honor wanted to be able to tell her what had happened to Melanie. She wanted to be able to give Candace information about where her mother was buried, offer to go with her to the grave even if that meant traveling to Texas or Florida to do so. Whatever Candace needed to do to find closure, that's what Honor wanted to offer.

But she wouldn't be able to offer anything at all if she didn't hurry up and call Chad. She frowned, dropping floured beef into the hot oil and browning it. Why was she being so wishy-washy about this? It wasn't like Chad was suddenly going to become part of their lives. He'd been more than happy to leave them alone for the past four years. There was no reason to think things had changed.

Was there?

Chad *had* just lost his wife. What if he felt the need to reconnect with the family he'd been so distant from?

A soft knock on the back door made Honor jump, and she turned to the sound, her pulse racing. "Who is it?"

"Grayson."

"What are you doing out in the rain?" Honor pulled the door open, surprised to see her neighbor.

Her friend?

More?

"Waiting for you to ask me in." He held a large black umbrella, but his hair was wet, his jacket speckled with raindrops.

"So come in."

"Something smells good." He left the umbrella in the mudroom and shrugged out of his coat, laying it over the back of the chair.

"I'm making stew for lunch."

"It's just a little past ten. Isn't it kind of early for lunch?"

"It takes time to make a good stew."

"I wouldn't know. I've never been much of a cook. Though I have to admit to a fondness for good, hearty stew." He moved toward the stove and looked down into the pot. "Is it beef stew?"

"Just like my mother use to make."

"Looks like what my mother use to make, too. There was nothing quite like it on a cold, rainy day." He was begging an invitation, but Honor wasn't sure issuing one would be the best way to protect her heart, so she just smiled, pouring broth over the beef and pretending she didn't notice.

"Mr. Sinclair!" Lily raced into the room, a page from her coloring book clutched in her hand. "Look what I made for you."

He took it, studying the brightly colored picture like it was a masterpiece and he an art connoisseur. "This is beautiful, Lily. I love the colors you used."

"The pink?"

"Yes. And the yellow, blue, green and purple." He glanced at Honor and smiled, including her in the exchange.

Her heart skipped a beat, and she turned her attention back to the stew, trying her best to ignore how kind Grayson was being to her daughter, how sweet his attention to the scribbled paper he'd received. Why did he have to be so perfect? Why couldn't he be impatient with Lily or unkind to Candace? At least then, she'd have an excuse besides cowardice to keep her distance.

"It's a gray day, so I used lots of colors. Like a rainbow. It's for you. See, I wrote your name on it."

Surprised, Honor glanced at the paper again. Lily was precocious for her age, reading books and copying words, but there was no way she could have known how to spell "Sinclair."

And of course, she hadn't.

She'd written "Mr. Prince" in bold letters at the bottom of the page, and Honor couldn't help smiling. "Didn't I tell you not to call him that, Lily Mae?"

"Yes, Mommy, but I couldn't spell his real name, so I had to write this one. I got it from the fairy-tale book Candace bought me."

Grayson laughed, ruffling Lily's hair and then folding the paper she'd given him and sliding it into his shirt pocket. "This is a great picture. Maybe you can color me another one for my brother. He hasn't been feeling well, so a picture like this might really cheer him up."

"Okay!" Lily skipped away, her curls flying in wild disarray. The room fell silent as she left it.

"I suppose you sent her out of here for a reason?" Honor pulled onions from the cupboard and started chopping them.

"I saw Jake at the courthouse an hour ago. He mentioned that he'd had some bad news to deliver to you, but wouldn't tell me what it was. I had to go home and grab the suit jacket I'd forgotten, so I figured I'd stop in here and see if things were okay."

"I'm surprised."

"By what?"

"The fact that Jake didn't tell you the news he'd given us."

"Don't be. Jake and I are both professionals who know the danger of crossing the line and letting personal relationships influence our actions."

"I know. I'm sorry. I didn't mean to imply anything different than that."

"And *I* know *that*." Grayson searched her face, his eyes sky blue and striking in his tan face. "So, *are* you okay?"

"I'm fine. It's Candace who is struggling. Jake was able to locate her parents. Or her father, anyway. Her mother passed away a couple of weeks ago."

"I'm sorry to hear that, Honor. Candace must be crushed."

"She is. I think the worst part for her is that her mother was gone for two weeks and she didn't even know it."

"Was there a reason why her father didn't contact you?"

"Who knows? I don't know Chad well, but what I know I don't like. He's a control freak given to fits of temper. Maybe he kept the information to himself out of spite. Maybe he did it because he could." Honor shrugged and threw the onions into the pot with the beef, then covered it with a lid.

"Is it possible he didn't know your new phone number? You did just recently move."

"We've had the same phone number for four years. If he'd dialed it, he would have been referred to our new number."

"Are you going to call him?"

"I've been trying to talk myself into getting that over with for the past hour and a half."

"You want me to do it for you?" Grayson frowned, pulling a cookie from the box sitting on Honor's counter.

"Grayson Sinclair, you'd better tell me that cookie isn't your breakfast."

"I would, but I'd be lying." He grinned and bit into the sweet treat.

"You need something more wholesome than that."

"If I had time, that's what I'd have, but I don't. I've got to be back in court in an hour."

"You shouldn't have come all the way here just to find out if everything was okay. You could have called me later."

"I told you—"

"You went back home for your suit jacket. Yes, I heard. But I can't believe a man like you doesn't keep a spare suit jacket at his office."

"Guilty as charged. But in my defense, I thought my black suit jacket would look better with the tie I'm wearing than my navy one."

"I wish you hadn't made the effort to stop by here, Grayson. Your day is already so hectic."

"I care. It's as simple as that." Grayson cupped her cheek. "So, do you want me to call your father-in-law?"

"No. That's a job I've got to do myself. And soon. Candace won't have closure until I give her the facts about what happened to her mother."

"Which just proves that kids can take a lot of abuse but still have loyalty and love for their parents." He grabbed another cookie and walked to the back door. "I've got to go or I'll be late. I'll be in court until this evening, and then I've got meetings tonight. If I'm not done in time to meet you after work—"

"I don't need you to meet me."

"If I'm not there, one of Jake's deputies will be. You've got a serious problem, Honor. Until we solve it, I think it's best to err on the side of caution."

He was right, of course. She couldn't take risks, not when she had Lily and Candace to think about. "All right."

"For once, we agree." He smiled, his gaze dropping to her lips and sending her heart racing before he met her eyes again. "Be safe on your way to work tonight."

"And you eat something besides junk food."

"I'm not making any promises." He called a goodbye to Lily, accepting the picture she'd colored for his brother with solemn thanks before he walked back out into the rain.

Honor stood at the door, watching as he crossed the yard and disappeared through the shrubs.

Talking to Grayson had eased some of the trepidation that had left her unable to pick up the phone and dial Chad's number. In his absence, Honor felt ready to do what she'd been putting off.

She grabbed the phone and dialed the number quickly, bracing herself for the conversation she was about to have.

"Hello?" Chad's voice was as gravelly and harsh as Honor remembered it to be.

"Chad. This is Honor Malone."

"Yeah, I thought you'd be calling after I talked to that sheriff. Guy asked me a couple hundred questions about Jay. Like I remember what my son was doing or who he was doing it with."

The crude statement made Honor wince, but she didn't comment. The easiest way to get along with Chad was to keep quiet and let him do all the talking.

Actually, that was the only way to get along with him.

"So, what do you want, Honor? I hope you're not going to try to get me to rescue you from whatever trouble you're in.

Seems to me there's been enough time between us that we aren't really family anymore."

"I didn't call to get your help, Chad. I called to find out what happened to Melanie. Candace needs to know."

"Then Candace should call herself."

"She's got a busy schedule."

"She's a coward. Just like Jay. The boy slunk away with his tail between his legs the minute he was old enough to leave home."

Honor gritted her teeth to keep from making a rude comment and tried to turn the conversation around. "Candace is in college. I know Melanie would be proud of her, and I'm sure you are, too."

"Melanie had her head in the booze too much to be proud of anyone or anything, but I've got to say it's good to know that my daughter didn't turn out like her worthless mother."

Charming. That was Chad. Unless he needed something from someone, he had no compassion—and showed it.

"Can you tell me what happened to Melanie? It really is important to Candace."

"What do you think happened to my wife? She drank herself to death."

"She died from alcohol poisoning?"

"She died of liver failure. Started having problems last year. Tried to quit drinking, but couldn't do it. Eventually her body just gave out."

"I'm sorry."

"So is everyone else I talk to."

"But not you?" The question slipped out, and Honor didn't regret it. Melanie's alcoholism had stolen her ability to mother effectively. As far as Honor could see, Chad had no excuse for being a poor father except sheer meanness.

"What I feel or don't feel isn't your business, Honor."

"But your reasons for not contacting us about Melanie are. Candace had a right to attend her mother's funeral."

"What funeral? Melanie wanted to be cremated and have her ashes scattered on the Gulf."

"Still—"

"Look, I'm pretty sure you mean well. You were always that kind of person. Too good for us Malones. But the fact is, it's over. Melanie is gone. I didn't contact Candace because after four years of never hearing from her, I didn't think she'd care to know. That might have been a mistake in judgment, but it wasn't a crime. So unless you've got something else you need to know, I've got to go."

"No. That's it."

"Good. Have a nice life, Honor." The phone clicked, the line disconnected, and Honor was left holding the phone and wondering how a man who had borne two children could have cared so little for them.

For all his faults, Jay had been immensely pleased by the idea of fatherhood. He'd planned a lifetime of father-child experiences before his death, and often talked to Honor about undoing the pattern of abuse his parents had created.

If he'd lived, he would have loved Lily desperately. Honor had no doubt about that.

She placed the phone back on the receiver, smiling at Lily who was watching her with wide, wary eyes.

"Well, that's that. I'm off the phone and I'm thinking we should make some of your grandmom's homemade bread to go with our stew. Want to help?"

"Okay."

"Get out the bread pans that are in the corner cupboard." Honor pulled yeast from a top shelf and started running warm water into a measuring cup. Angry for Candace's sake, but unable to do anything with the emotion, she concentrated her efforts on kneading soft white dough, pounding it and imagining it was her father-in-law's aristocratic nose she was hitting.

TWENTY

The sky was already lightening, the first hints of morning turning it deep cerulean as Grayson drove past the police cruiser stationed at the end of Honor's street. He waved to the officer as he drove by, then turned his attention to Honor's small bungalow. Her car was parked in the driveway just as it should be. Satisfied and relieved, Grayson drove around the corner and pulled into his own driveway.

His muscles ached from tension, and his eyes were dry from fatigue, but he'd won two court cases, guaranteeing that two very bad men would be in prison for a long time. He'd also met with his team and planned out a strategy for a high-profile case that was on the docket. It had taken hours, but everything he'd wanted to accomplish had been done. Now he was home for a quick shower, some food and a catnap before he started the routine all over again.

The morning was silent, the cold clear air giving Grayson a quick burst of energy as he hurried to his front door. It was false energy, but at least it was energy. He'd been dragging since he'd returned from New York. Emotional stress, worry about Jude. Worry about Honor and her family. All those things had made sleeping difficult. The part of him that had been raised to believe that God was in control, the part of him that *did* believe it, rebelled at the idea of losing sleep over worry. If God was in control, He'd work everything out according to His plan. There was no reason to spend time worrying about it.

Of course, Grayson wasn't the kind to let others do what he thought he could. Even in his relationship with God, he often spent more time solving his own problems than waiting for God to do it. He was a man of action, and he'd never seen anything wrong with that until recently. Lately, he was trying to back off and let God take control. It wasn't easy, but he had no choice. As much as he wanted to put an end to Honor's nightmare, he couldn't.

That was a hard pill to swallow, but a necessary one.

Honor had said it best—until a person realized faith was all he had, he couldn't understand that it was all he needed.

Grayson ran a hand over his hair and yawned. He'd been up for almost twenty-four hours. He needed to rectify that situation. Now. He was going inside. He was going to lie down. And he was going to forget about everything for two hours.

He walked up the steps that led to his front door, pausing when he caught sight of a white plastic grocery bag hanging from the door handle. Not a cosmetic catalogue or advertisement, as the contents were larger and thicker. So what was it?

Grayson approached cautiously, mindful of the threat that had been made against him. The man stalking Honor could easily have visited Grayson's house while the police sat around the corner. He eyed the bag, leaning close, trying to see its contents. Anything electrical and he'd call Jake, have him send for the state's bomb squad.

The scent of yeast hung in the air near the bag. And something else. Onions. Beef.

Stew?

He lifted the bag, peered inside and saw a clear plastic container filled with what looked like stew. Three thick slices of bread were in a plastic Ziploc bag, and Grayson's mouth watered at the sight. He hadn't realized how hungry he was until that moment. Now he was starving. There was a folded piece of paper inside the bag, and he pulled it out as he went in to the house and flicked on the foyer light.

Grayson, I decided to help you out on your quest for more nutritious food and brought some beef stew for you. Lily and I made the bread together. If you clean your plate, there are a few chocolate-chip cookies packed, too. Honor.

Grayson smiled as he read the note. He doubted Honor had meant for him to eat the stew at this time of the day, but it looked too good to pass up. Besides, he'd sleep better on a full stomach. He heated the stew up in the microwave, his gaze drawn again and again to the sunroom windows that looked out over the back yard. Honor's house was dark for a change, but Grayson still wanted to walk outside, cross the yard and go over to see her. It seemed odd that after such a short amount of time, Honor would have become so deeply entrenched in his thoughts.

He'd dated Maria for two years before he'd proposed, because he had firmly believed it took at least that long to get to know someone.

Had firmly believed that.

Now he wasn't quite as sure.

Despite the short amount of time he'd known Honor, he

knew her goals and dreams, knew what she valued and what she didn't. Knew that being with her was the most comfortable part of his day. Knew that being without her made him long to be near her again.

He'd always scoffed at the idea of love at first sight. His relationship with Maria had been about mutual benefit more than deep emotion. In retrospect, that seemed like a cold and calculated reason to plan a marriage, but at the time it had made sense. Maria was an attractive, intelligent woman whose goals and aspirations had been similar to Grayson's. After weighing the pros and cons, balancing risk with benefit, Grayson had decided that marriage with her would be worth it.

Maria's response hadn't been any less deliberate. There'd been no tearful acceptance. No speechless nod. Maria had slipped the ring on her finger, leaned forward to plant a chaste kiss on Grayson's lips and announced that their marriage would be the perfect merger.

Merger?

Was it any wonder their relationship hadn't worked out?

With Honor things were different. With her, the relationship was more about emotional need and support than convenience. The kisses they'd shared had burned into his soul, branding his heart in a way no other woman's ever had.

He frowned, spooning up a mouthful of rich stew, and acknowledging a truth he'd been avoiding. He'd spent years maintaining careful control in every area of his life. His days planned, his schedule carefully worked out, his life's goals clearly defined. College, law school, a career as a state prosecutor. He'd had a time line for all those things. As well as for relationships, marriage and kids. He hadn't wanted his careful plans ruined. Hadn't wanted the messy complications a relationship could bring. He'd liked his life just the way it had been.

Until he'd met Honor.

One look in her eyes and he'd seen forever.

He wouldn't let a deranged stalker take that from him.

Honor stifled a yawn and glanced at her watch as she stepped out of a patient's room. Ten more minutes and her shift would end. Good. She'd been distracted and ill at ease for most of the day. Speaking with her father-in-law the previous day had added more anxiety to the boiling cauldron that had taken up residence in her stomach. The fact that she hadn't seen Grayson since the previous afternoon had nothing to do with her sour mood. Nothing at all.

"What's wrong with you?" Will fell into step beside her as she moved down the hall.

"Nothing. Why?"

"Because you've spent the entire shift looking like your best friend died."

"Actually, my mother-in-law did."

"Yeah? I'm sorry to hear that, Honor."

"Me, too."

"Maybe we could go out for a drink or something to take the edge off our troubles."

"That's not my kind of thing."

"I didn't think so, but I thought I'd ask anyway. So, how about we just go get something to eat? A little post-dinner/pre-breakfast meal?"

"How about we just do what we always do? Walk out to our cars together and say good-night."

"If I didn't know better, I'd think you were a cold-hearted witch."

"Will!" Surprised, Honor took a hard look at her co-worker. He'd always seemed benign if persistent, but maybe he was something a lot more sinister than that.

"Hey, I'm kidding."

"It didn't sound like a joke."

"Sorry. I've had a long day. Maybe it's coming out in my tone." But he didn't sound sorry, and Honor wondered if walking out to her car with him was a good idea.

Was it possible Will was her stalker?

She'd bring up the idea to Jake. For now, she'd go on instinct and leave without him. Either Grayson or a police cruiser had been waiting for her after work for the past few nights. She'd be safe enough walking outside on her own.

As soon as her shift ended, she signed out, hurrying from the nurse's station before Will arrived from his rounds. The night was dark and silent, the moon a golden crescent. Honor scanned the parking lot as she hurried through it, searching for and finding Grayson's car in its usual spot at the far end of the lot.

Relieved, she offered a quick wave and got into her car, starting the engine and glancing in her rearview mirror, her heart stopping as she saw a face staring back at her. Dark gleaming eyes. Pale distorted features.

The face in the window.

Something hard and smooth pressed against the back of her head and Honor froze. Afraid to move. Afraid to breathe.

"I've got a gun, Honor. I'd hate to have to use it." He spoke in a harsh whisper. A voice that could be anyone or no one. The voice of every nightmare, every fear she'd ever had.

"Who are you? What do you want?" Honor's voice trembled, her mind blank but for one thought—she was going to die.

"We'll talk about that later. Right now, we need to get away from your friend. He's really become a problem, don't you think?"

"What are you planning?"

"Just some alone-time with you. So, here's what you're going to do. You're going to drive over to where he's parked, and you're going to unroll your window and get him to do the same. Then you're going to tell him that you're sick of being followed around. You're going to accuse him of being your stalker. You're going to tell him that if he follows you home again, you're going to file a restraining order against him."

"He'll never believe that."

"He'd better. I didn't bring the gun to use on you, Honor. Though I will, if I have to. I brought it to take care of anyone who tries to stop me from going after what I want. So, you'd better make sure you're convincing. I'd hate to see an attorney's brains splattered all over the pavement before we go off on our adventure."

"You don't know Grayson. There's nothing I could say that would convince him to—"

"I know *everything*." The hissed words shivered through Honor and made her mouth go dry with fear. The hard nudge of the gun butting against her head filled her with the kind of terror she'd felt only once before. Then she'd been saved by a neighbor. This time, she might not be saved at all.

"Please…"

"Listen to me, I know your prosecutor friend won't risk his career over you. All you have to do is convince him that pursuing his hero-fantasy might cost him that. He'll take off, and we can be on our way in peace. Come on. Drive. If you take too long and he comes over to investigate, things might get messy. You won't like messy."

Did she have a choice?

Honor couldn't think of one. At least not one that ended with her alive. She put the car in gear, her legs trembling so much she pressed too hard on the accelerator and the car jumped forward, the butt of the gun knocking into her head again.

"Better watch it. These things can go off easily. I'm going to get out of sight, but this gun is pressed right against the back of your seat. It'll be easy enough to make you sorry if I have to."

Honor's teeth chattered, but she did what she'd been told—drive over to Grayson's car, motion for him to roll down his window.

He smiled a welcome and did as she'd indicated, speaking softly into the silent darkness. "Hey, looks like you're out a little earlier tonight."

"Yes. I decided not to wait for Will."

"Didn't I tell you not to walk outside by yourself?"

"Yes." Her mind was blank, her body frozen with fear. She couldn't think of what she was supposed to say. She couldn't remember what she had to do to save Grayson and herself.

"Is everything okay, Honor?" Grayson shifted and Honor was sure he was going to get out of his car, see the madman in the back seat of her Ford and die. She wouldn't let that be the last thing she ever saw. She wouldn't let his life end so brutally.

"It's fine. Just fine. The thing is..." A hard jab at her back urged her on. "I'm getting tired of being followed home every night."

"It's for your own safety."

"I'm beginning to wonder if that's really the truth. I'm beginning to think something else is going on."

"What?" He frowned, and Honor knew he had no idea the direction she was heading in.

"Everything was fine in Lakeview, Grayson, until you came home from New York."

His expression tightened, his frown turning to a scowl. "What are you implying, Honor?"

"I'm not implying anything. I'm flat-out saying it." Her voice was rising with her mounting fear. He'd hear it as anger. She only hoped it would convince him to drive away.

"I don't think I'm clear on what exactly you are saying. Maybe you can fill me in on a few more details."

"I met you and within twenty-four hours I started receiving flowers and threats."

"So?"

"So how do I know that you're not the one responsible? How do I know that you didn't see me that first day and decide you'd do whatever it took to have me?"

His laughter was harsh and ugly, his eyes flashing with anger. "You have got to be kidding me."

"Kidding? I'm dead serious."

"Honor, you received a phone call from the stalker while I was with you. Don't you think it would have been difficult for me to make it while you were standing next to me?" The question was as harsh as his laugh had been, his eyes narrowing as he stared her down.

"You know plenty of criminals. I'm sure one of them would have been willing to make the phone call for the right price."

"I think we'd better end this conversation. I'll be happy to discuss the subject again when we've both had some sleep. For now, I'll make sure you get home safely, and then I'll get out of your life."

"Get rid of him now, or he gets it." The soft whisper from behind Honor was like a cobra's hiss—filled with deadly promise.

"I already told you I'm tired of being followed. If you choose to ignore that, I'll be forced to file an order of protection against you."

"Have you lost your mind?" Grayson bit the words out and Honor knew she'd done what she'd intended. She wanted to beg Grayson's forgiveness, she wanted to tell him it was all a lie.

"No, but I better have lost my tail. I *will* file the order, Grayson, so don't follow me." She rolled up her window and drove away, glancing in the rearview mirror, tears in her eyes.

Had he sensed her fear?

Did he realize how many lies she'd told?

Did he know how much she cared about him?

"Crying for your lover, Honor?" The man behind her sneered, rearing up from behind the seat and pressing his gun against her cheek.

"Grayson is my friend."

"That kiss you gave him looked more than friendly."

The words left her cold. He'd been watching even when she'd thought she was safe.

"Is he following us?" The disembodied voice was louder, the serpent sounding more like a self-satisfied man than a cobra.

"No."

"Good. I didn't want to ruin our party if I didn't have to." His masked face appeared in the mirror again, and Honor cringed. "You must be a good actress, Honor. He seemed completely convinced. But I'm not surprised. You've got so many other good qualities."

"Let me go. Please."

"You're going to beg? I expected so much more from you." The cold barrel of the gun ran down the side of her neck, and Honor had to force herself to keep breathing.

"I'm not begging."

"Sure you are. But it won't do you any good. We've got a date with destiny."

"Where are we going?"

"Into the mountains. You know the Blue Ridge Parkway, right?"

"Yes."

"Drive toward it."

"What happens when we get there?"

"I'll let you know when it's time."

"But—"

"Drive!" The gun butted hard into her cheek, and Honor knew that the night was going to get a lot worse before it got better.

If it ever got better.

She shivered, keeping her gaze straight ahead and praying desperately for the help she was afraid would never come.

TWENTY-ONE

Grayson waited a few heartbeats before pulling out after Honor. He kept his headlights off and his speed down, not wanting Honor to know he was behind her. Not because he believed she'd file an order of protection against him, but because she was a bad actress. So bad that he'd known before she even began speaking that something was very wrong. She'd said all the right things, but he'd seen the fear in her eyes. Had known what it meant.

Someone had been in the car with her.

That was the only explanation he could come up with for the stark terror she'd shown in her eyes and for her bizarre accusation. His hands tightened on the steering wheel and his heart beat furiously as he followed her car.

He'd had another late meeting and had intended to have a police officer escort her home again, but worry had nagged at his gut, pulled at his attention, demanded that he be the one to make sure she arrived home safely.

It wasn't often Grayson saw evidence of God's intervention, but this was one of those times. It would have been easy for Honor to send a police officer on his way. She then would have driven off with a madman in her car and no one would have been the wiser. Not until her girls woke up to her absence, or her body was found beaten and bloodied on the side of some road.

And there was no doubt in Grayson's mind that that was exactly what her stalker planned to do. He'd seen it before. Seen the photographs of crime scenes as he tried men who'd created elaborate fantasies, been disappointed and killed the object of their affection.

He wouldn't let that happen to Honor.

He pulled his cell phone from the console, started to dial 911, but hesitated. If some gung-ho cop came riding to the rescue with lights flashing and sirens blaring, Honor would be dead before he ever made it to her car. He dialed Jake's cell phone, instead.

"Reed here."

"Jake, it's Grayson. We've got a situation on the Blue Ridge Parkway."

"Tell me."

Grayson explained as succinctly as possible, refusing to give in to the anger and fear that were surging through him.

"You're on the Parkway, now?"

"Heading toward the overlook."

"I'm on my way. You back off and let us handle this." Jake issued the order, but Grayson chose not to hear it.

"What's your ETA?"

"Fifteen minutes."

"A lot can happen in fifteen minutes."

"Back off. If you don't, you're going to get in our way and slow us down."

"If I do, Honor might not be alive when you finally get to her. I'll call you if things change."

"Don't—"

Grayson hung up. He was done talking. Done with rational conversation. They were dealing with irrationality. Stalkers weren't working with a full deck. They acted in ways that couldn't be predicted. Grayson wasn't willing to step back and wait for the guy who was with Honor to make a move.

He pressed down on the gas, closing the distance between his car and Honor's. If something happened, he wanted to be close enough to stop it.

Honor gripped the steering wheel with both hands, her heart pounding at an alarming pace. If she had a heart attack, the car would go over the side of the mountain. She and her nightmare would tumble head over heels until they hit the earth below.

Death. Quick and swift and hopefully painless.

Something told her that wasn't what the masked man behind her had planned.

"There's a scenic overlook up ahead. Follow the signs and drive there. Park the car."

"What are we—"

"We'll talk when we get there."

"If we're going to talk, we should go somewhere warmer. Maybe a nice romantic restaurant." If he really had some kind of fantasy about having a relationship with Honor, maybe he'd like the idea of having dinner with her better than the idea of brutally murdering her and throwing her off the side of the mountain.

She shuddered at the thought.

"Dinner at a restaurant? Why not just go back to your place? You've certainly been entertaining that lawyer there plenty."

"I wasn't—"

"Shut up." The gun pressed against her cheek, jabbing hard enough to bring tears to Honor's eyes.

She did what she was told, her gaze darting to the rearview mirror. She expected to see her captor staring back at her, but saw only the open road.

Or was it?

Had there been something moving in the distance? She looked in the mirror again, her breath catching in her throat as she realized a car was coming up behind them. Lights off, but still visible in the moonlight. Was it the police? She'd been praying desperately that Grayson hadn't fallen for her act, praying that he'd realized something was wrong and called for help.

"The turn is coming up. Don't miss it or we'll have our chat somewhere a lot less comfortable."

Honor jerked her attention back to the road and took the turn a little too quickly. Her tires squealed and slid, and Honor gripped the steering wheel hard, terror filling her. She didn't want to die. Not now. She had too many things to do with her life. Too many memories she still wanted to create.

Please, Lord, don't let me die.

"This is it. Pull into the parking area and turn off the car."

Terror thrummed through Honor's veins, her heart pounding so fast she thought it would leap from her chest, but she did what she was told. She'd fight when she had to. Until then, she'd do everything she could to stay alive.

"Good. Now, we're getting out of the car nice and slow. You try to run and I'll shoot you in the back. Understand?"

"I won't try to run." Yet.

"That's what I wanted to hear. Give me your keys and get out."

She pulled the keys from the ignition, her hand shaking as she placed them in his. He was wearing gloves. She hadn't realized it until now. And she knew beyond a shadow of a doubt that she was about to die.

She got out of the car anyway. Her chances were going to be better outside.

"Walk over to that little railing. The one that looks out over the valley. I picked this spot especially for you."

"I'm afraid of heights." It was a lie she could live with. One that she hoped would keep her far away from any place where she could be thrown off.

"Are you? Funny, I heard you climbed rock walls in college and dreamed of making a trek to Mount Everest."

That *had* been a dream of hers years ago, and hearing it now made her cringe. "How do you know that?"

"I know everything there is to know about you, Honor. And I know everything there is to know about how to keep what's rightfully mine."

"I'm not yours."

He laughed, his breath hot and clammy against her ear. "You? Did you really believe this was about *you?* You're nothing, Honor. Nothing but some transplant from Ireland who thinks she's better than everyone." His voice changed as he spoke, the harsh whisper replaced by something familiar. Something she'd heard less than twenty-four hours ago.

"Chad?" She pivoted toward him, saw a flash of movement.

Pain exploded through her head, driving everything away until there was only darkness and the soft, sweet feel of oblivion.

Grayson lunged forward as the man who'd hit Honor leaned down and grabbed her arms.

He didn't give the guy a chance to react, just grasped him

by the back of the shirt and yanked him around, punching him in the abdomen. Not caring about the gun that clattered to the ground. Not caring about anything but protecting Honor.

The man grunted, his breath leaving on a whoosh of sound. Grayson hit him again, this time in the face. Hearing the satisfying crack of bone against bone, the thud of flesh slamming into flesh.

Honor's attacker stumbled backward, landing in a heap, but then stumbling to his feet again, he turned, trying to run. Grayson lunged forward, grabbing his arm and jerking him around, ready to punch him again.

His hand was grabbed mid-swing, the force of the restraint stopping his momentum. "You'd better cool it, friend. We don't want any charges of police brutality." Jake Reed's voice was as calm as a placid lake, but there was steel in his grip.

"I'm not the police."

"You're the prosecutor. We don't need you getting into trouble, either."

"I don't really care what kind of trouble I get into."

"One punch to the guy, I can ignore. I can't ignore two, Gray. And you're not going to do Honor any good if I've got to cart you away and lock you up for a twelve-hour cool-down."

The words finally registered through the red haze of his fury, and Grayson released his hold on the man. Stepped back, turned away.

Honor lay on her side on the ground, her hair covering her face. Grayson knelt beside her, joining a female deputy who was checking Honor's pulse. "Is she okay?"

"Her pulse is strong and steady, but she's out cold. I'm going to call for transport to Lynchburg General." The deputy stood, speaking into her radio as she hovered nearby.

Grayson ignored her, focusing his attention on Honor. He brushed thick strands of silky hair from her face and saw blood on her temple. "Honor?"

His fingers grazed her cheek, dropped to her neck to check her pulse again. As his hand moved, Honor's eyes opened. Hazy. Confused. But open.

"Grayson. You came."

"Did you think I wouldn't?" Relief made his hand shake as he leaned in to help Honor sit up. He slipped a hand behind her back, supporting her when she swayed.

"I told you not to."

"And you expected me to listen?"

"I hoped you wouldn't. I prayed you wouldn't."

"And I prayed that God would help me keep you safe."

"I guess we both got what we prayed for." She smiled, wincing a little as she turned her head. "It *is* Chad."

"What?" He stared into her eyes, trying to determine if the head injury was causing her confusion.

"My stalker. It's Chad Malone."

"Your father-in-law?" He looked at the man he'd punched. Short, stocky, cropped brown hair and angry, hate-filled eyes.

"Yes. I just can't figure out why he'd want to hurt me, or how he ended up here."

"Jake will find out soon enough."

"Good. My head hurts too much to try to work it out myself." She leaned a little more heavily on his arm, and Grayson tightened his hold, calling out to the female deputy.

"Is the ambulance on the way?"

"It should be here in ten."

"Ambulance. For what?" Honor's voice sounded much

weaker than Grayson liked, and the blood from her head wound was beginning to pool on the pavement.

"For you."

"I don't need an ambulance."

"You're bleeding like a stuck pig. You do need an ambulance." Grayson pulled off his coat, using the sleeve to staunch the flow of blood.

"Head wounds always bleed a lot."

"Yeah? Well, from the looks of things, you're going to need stitches. You've got a two-inch gash in your temple." He brushed hair away from the spot, lifting the coat to look at the wound. "It's deep."

"It'll have to wait. I need to get home to the girls."

"I'll call Candace and tell her what happened."

"No!" Honor lowered her voice. "She'll panic."

"Then I'll just tell her you got held up. You can explain things when you get home."

"Explain? I don't even understand what happened."

"I'll go see if Jake has any information." He started to rise, but Honor grabbed his hand, holding him in place.

"Don't go. I need to thank you before I forget."

"Thank me for what?"

"For slaying the dragon." She smiled, her pale face beautiful in the moonlight.

"I didn't slay him. I wanted to, though."

"You did slay him, and I can't wait to tell Lily what I learned tonight."

"What's that?"

"That you really are a prince." She laid a palm against his cheek, urging him closer and placing a kiss on his lips.

Grayson laughed, relief and happiness stripping away

anger and fear. Hope replacing anxiety. He didn't know what the next few hours would bring, had no idea what would happen over the course of Jake's investigation, but he knew Honor was going to be okay.

That was enough for now.

TWENTY-TWO

Honor stared at her reflection in the bathroom mirror and grimaced, wishing she hadn't agreed to go out. She had looked bad enough after a few sleepless nights. Add fifteen stitches and a bruised cheekbone and her face was shudder-worthy.

Someone knocked at the front door, and Honor froze, her heart pounding with anticipation and dread. She'd been imagining this moment all day. Now that it was here, she wasn't sure she was ready for it.

Lily's squeals of excitement told Honor that Candace had opened the door and let their visitor in.

"Is Honor ready?" Grayson's voice carried down the hall, and Honor glanced at her reflection one last time.

Was she ready?

"I'll be right there." She dusted powder over her bruised cheek, pulled hair over the stitches and prayed Grayson wouldn't take one look at her and change his mind about their date.

Honor's first in over eight years.

Just the thought made her stomach churn.

"Honor, come on. Mr. Sinclair is waiting." Candace appeared at the bathroom door looking as nervous as Honor felt. "You look beautiful, so stop staring at yourself and go."

"Maybe I should cancel."

"Are you nuts? That man is the best thing that has happened in your life since I moved in with you."

Her words made Honor laugh, and she winced as her cheek throbbed in response.

Two days after Chad had attacked her, and she was just beginning to heal. She could only hope Candace's emotional wounds were doing the same.

She studied her sister-in-law's face, trying to find some clue as to how the teenager was doing. But Candace looked the same as always—sweet and just a little closed off, her expression impossible to read. "Are you sure you don't mind me going out tonight?"

"Are you kidding? I've been praying you'd hook up with Grayson since the first time I saw him."

"You have not."

"I have, too. Now come on. Before he decides you're taking too long and leaves."

"Candace…" She wasn't sure what she wanted to say, but only knew it was there, just below the surface, waiting to be revealed.

"Honor." Candace used the same inflection Honor had, her eyes sparkling with humor and hiding whatever grief she might be feeling. Then she sobered, putting her hand on Honor's arm. "You don't have to worry about me, you know."

"Of course, I do. I love you."

"And I love you, too." It was the first time she'd ever said the words, and Honor's eyes burned with tears she didn't dare shed. "But love doesn't mean worry. It means prayer. And with your prayers over me, I'll be just fine."

"What your father did was awful, but it had nothing to do with you. You know that, right?"

"It had plenty to do with me. He wanted control of the trust funds Mom had left to me and Lily. He was willing to kill you to make sure he got it." Candace's jaw tightened, but she didn't walk away as she had every other time Honor had broached the subject.

"Which had nothing to do with you."

"Honor, a man whose DNA I share waited until Mom was getting ready to take her last breath and then hired a doped-up druggie to kill you in St. Louis. When that failed, he decided to 'stalk' and kill you, figuring the police would never suspect him of the crime. If he had succeeded, he would have effectively gotten rid of the trustee to Mom's estate which was the only thing that stood between him and two million dollars."

"He didn't succeed, though."

"Not for lack of trying. And the way he just blabbed it all out hoping for a plea bargain? What a coward." Candace stepped back, her expression closed off again. "You really need to get moving. Lily is probably making Mr. Sinclair crazy. Ever since you told her he really was a dragon slayer and said you'd seen him slay a dragon, she won't stop pestering him to tell the story."

"Grayson will be okay for another minute."

"Honor, please, just go." The tears in Candace's eyes were unmistakable, and Honor wanted desperately to pull her into a hug.

She knew she'd be rebuffed, so she patted her shoulder instead. "I really don't want to leave you, Candace."

"And I already told you that you don't need to worry. Go have dinner and enjoy being with a handsome man."

"I—"

"Honor, is everything okay?" Grayson stood in the hallway, his hair brushed back from his forehead, his gaze touching on her bruised cheek, then resting on her lips before he met her eyes. Her heart jumped in acknowledgment, all the anxiety she'd been feeling melting away.

"Everything is fine. I'm just not sure I should leave Candace…and Lily home tonight."

"Then we'll order pizza or Chinese and eat it here." He brushed strands of hair from her cheek, his fingers lingering, his touch heating her skin.

"No, you won't!" Candace protested loudly, but Grayson just smiled in her direction.

"Sorry, kid. You're outvoted."

"This is ridiculous. I'm not a baby, you know. I don't need a sitter." Candace huffed the words and stomped away, her disgust obvious.

"Do you think she'll get over it?" Grayson tugged Honor a few steps down the hall, stopping before they got to the living room and wrapping his arms around her waist, his scent and his warmth as familiar as an old friend.

"Get over us not going out for dinner? Yes. Get over what her father did? I don't know." Honor sighed and snuggled close to his chest.

"It must be tough for her, knowing that her father is a murderer."

"Chad didn't actually kill anyone." And Honor liked to tell herself he wouldn't have. That either she would have escaped, or he would have changed his mind. She knew the truth, though. Chad would have done anything to gain control of what he thought was rightfully his—the money his wife had inherited from her parents and had kept out of his hands for their entire marriage. It was the one thing he had never been able to take from her. The one thing he'd been determined to get.

No matter the cost.

As soon as he'd realized that Melanie would not be leaving him anything in her will, he'd begun plotting. When hospice had been called in to care for his ailing wife, he'd set his plan in motion, hiring a druggie to kill Honor. Jake and Grayson both suspected that he planned to kill the man after the fact.

Honor preferred not to speculate on any of her father-in-law's plans.

When his attempt to have Honor murdered had failed, Chad had decided to take matters into his own hands. Stalking Honor became a game that he learned to play well. His phone calls were forwarded from his house in Florida to his cell phone, and neither Jake nor Honor had realized he was in Lakeview until it was almost too late. If he hadn't slipped and mentioned Jay's infidelity they might never have made the connection to him. Whether or not Jake's phone call had forced Chad's hand and made him act earlier than he'd planned, was something Chad refused to discuss.

He'd certainly been willing to discuss just about everything else. Like Candace had said, he'd spilled everything, hoping for leniency that Grayson was determined to see he never got.

And rightfully so.

Just thinking about the terrifying ride up into the mountains made Honor shiver.

"Hey, are you okay?" Grayson cupped her face, his hands anchoring her to the present, his eyes beckoning her into the future. And she knew she would risk her heart to go there with him.

"With you here, how could I not be?"

He smiled, pressing a kiss to her lips, the touch so gentle a tear slipped down her cheek.

"Don't cry." His rough palm smoothed away the moisture.

"How can I not when I'm so happy?"

He kissed her again, stealing her breath and filling her heart so that there was no room for regrets or sorrow.

"Mommy? Is this the part in the story when the prince gets to kiss the princess and they live happily ever after?" Lily's voice cut into the moment, and Grayson pulled away, smiling down into Honor's eyes, offering her everything she'd ever wanted.

"Yes, Lily Mae. It most definitely is." And she pulled Grayson's head down for another kiss, sealing the moment and their future together.

Dear Reader,

Honor Malone's character was inspired by my grandmother, a widow who raised five children alone. Nana poured her heart, soul and passion into her kids. Perhaps that was why she never remarried. Like my grandmother, Honor is a strong, determined mother who has no intention of marrying again after her first husband dies. Despite her deep faith in God, she doesn't want to acknowledge that Grayson Sinclair might be part of His perfect plan for her life. I hope you enjoy reading Honor and Grayson's story, and I pray that wherever you are heading, God will be the compass that guides you on your journey.

If you have time, drop me a line at: shirlee@shirleemccoy.com or by mail at P.O. Box 592, Gambrills, MD 21054.

All His best,

Shirlee McCoy

QUESTIONS FOR DISCUSSION

1. Why is Honor so determined to remain single?

2. In what way did Honor's marriage to Jay change her perspective on life?

3. How did that change affect her relationship with her daughter, her sister-in-law and even with God?

4. How would you describe Honor's relationship with God?

5. Honor is a strong woman who doesn't want to need anyone. What is it about Grayson that makes her want to rely on him?

6. Grayson has spent years pursuing his career. What things has he put on hold in order to be successful?

7. Grayson has been a Christian for many years, but his relationship with God has waned. Have there been times in your life when you've felt distant from God? What things in your life draw you away from a close relationship with Him?

8. What steps does Grayson take to reclaim his relationship with God?

9. Grayson has put aside the thought of marriage and family, but meeting Honor makes him wonder if both might once

again be possible. How does his renewed relationship with God strengthen his resolve to pursue a relationship with Honor?

10. Trust is an underlying theme in Honor and Grayson's story. Why is it so hard for Honor to trust Grayson?

11. Honor's relationship with Grayson isn't the only thing that changes during the course of the story. How does Honor's faith grow during her troubles?

12. Honor has difficulty believing that Grayson is part of God's plan for her life. Have you ever struggled to understand the truth of God's plan? How were you able to finally understand what He wanted for your life?